Joanna Bolouri worked in sales before she began writing professionally at the age of thirty. Winning a BBC comedy script competition allowed her to work and write with stand-up comedians, comedy scriptwriters and actors from across the UK. She's had articles and reviews published in *The Skinny*, the Scottish *Sun*, the *Huffington Post* and *Heckler-Spray*. She lives in Glasgow with her daughter.

Also by Joanna Bolouri

The List
I Followed the Rules
The Most Wonderful Time of the Year
Relight My Fire
All I Want for Christmas

Driving Home for Christmas

JOANNA BOLOURI

QUERCUS

First published in Great Britain in 2022 by

QUERCUS

Quercus Editions Ltd
Carmelite House
50 Victoria Embankment
London EC4Y 0DZ

An Hachette UK company

A CIP catalogue record for this book is available
from the British Library

PB ISBN 978 1 52942 146 0

10 9 8 7 6 5 4 3 2 1

Typeset by CC Book Production
Printed and bound in Great Britain by Clays Ltd, Elcograf S.p.A.

Papers used by Quercus are from well-managed forests and other responsible sources.

For Mum, Dad, Claudia, Olivia, Matias and Valentina

DECEMBER 23RD

Ed

I'm sorry! Five more minutes, I promise! xx

Five more minutes. She said that ten minutes ago.

In fact, she first said it forty-five minutes ago when I still had some feeling left in my fingers and couldn't see my own breath every time I sighed with exasperation. She also told me she'd *absolutely, definitely, one million per cent* be ready to leave work at six-thirty to make the drive to my parents' house, and yet here I am at seven-thirty – alone in my freezing car, with the engine turned off so I don't drain the battery.

I glare up at the office block, towards Kate's window on the fifth floor, hoping a stern look might somehow motivate her to leave sooner. God, this building is depressing. It looks like a Victorian workhouse with walls of intimidating, uninspiring brown brick and windows all separated into smaller glass sections, resembling prison bars, even with the tasteful Christmas decorations outlining each frame. The whole ghastly structure surrounds a private one-hour-a-day-of-exercise-like courtyard which is now a private car park for brand-new-Mercedes-owning staff only and not their disgruntled boyfriends who drive 2012 Volkswagen Golfs. Unlike the contemporary, shiny, glass buildings popping up all over London, this one is considerably less modern . . . bleak, even. Kate doesn't share my views. That's not entirely unfamiliar these days.

I'm given a momentary burst of optimism as I see someone peer out of the window, and hope to glimpse a flash of her red hair, but although Kate's been up there long enough to grow a beard, I'm guessing it's not her. Come to think of it, I'm not even certain that *is* her window; she's worked at Parish Scott Taylor for three years, but I've never actually set foot inside her office. Lately, I get the feeling Kate wishes she hadn't either.

'They're just so bloody . . . agghh! These people! These rich, privileged arseholes trying to nit-pick over every tiny detail of their divorce because god forbid their soon-to-be ex-spouse gets custody of the integrated dishwasher or the silver corn-on-the-cob forks. I mean, who the fuck even owns corn-on-the-cob forks? Arseholes, that's who.'

My attention turns from the bushy-faced man towards the end of the road, where the streets are packed with people who keep normal working hours, heading to places which are undoubtedly warmer than this bloody car. We're pretty close to Camden and right now I'd give anything to be sat in the Blues Kitchen with some St Louis ribs and a beer, instead of contemplating what pre-packed sandwich meal deal I'll get when we inevitably stop at motorway services because Kate will have been mainlining coffee all day.

A loud, sharp rap on the passenger window nearly gives me a heart attack.

'Open up, it's freezing out here!'

I lean across and unlock the door, as a flustered-looking Kate climbs into the passenger seat.

'God, I'm so sorry, honey!' she exclaims, throwing her work bag into the back seat. 'I got stuck with a client that Baroness Botox decided would be more comfortable with me instead of Julian because we come from the same part of the world. But we don't. Well, not unless Newcastle has suddenly become part of the Peak District, and no one's told me.'

Her freckled face is flushed as she kicks off her shoes and throws them into the back to join her work bag. I can't imagine what it's like having to walk around in those all day. Like trying to balance on very small, pointy stilts.

She leans back into her seat and sighs as I turn on the engine. 'It's colder in here than it is outside,' she remarks. 'You should have kept the car running.'

'For an hour?' I reply frowning. 'You know how temperamental Kiki is. She'd have lost the will to live before we hit the motorway.'

'Well, I did suggest taking my Mini,' she replies, her

eyes darting upwards in disapproval. She finds car naming ridiculous. 'I just had it serviced last week.'

'Yes, but it also has the boot capacity of a pencil case,' I respond, fiddling with the heater control. 'You'd be lucky to get two overnight bags in there, never mind the mountains of gifts you've bought for—'

'Let's just go, shall we? We're late as it is.'

I bite my tongue as I put on my seatbelt, indicate and move off. I know she's stressed at work right now but honestly, sometimes she can be a complete pain in the—

'Ed! Watch out!'

I slam on the brakes as a cyclist appears from nowhere, narrowly missing my car. Mouthing obscenities at me, he rides off, while I give him a commonly recognised one-fingered gesture.

'Didn't you see him? Bloody hell, Ed, be more careful.'

'Me?' I reply, in astonishment. 'That was his fault. It's a one-way street.'

I exhale loudly and pull away again, just as a fox decides to dart across the road in front of us, disappearing into the nearby public square garden.

'For the love of god!' I exclaim. 'I'm going to have a heart attack before we even get to the end of the street.'

Kate laughs and puts her hand on my knee, which soothes me a little. 'Third time lucky?' she asks.

I nod and move off again, checking every blind spot

twice. Part of me wants to get out and check the sky for rogue parachuters.

'All good with directions?' Kate asks, as we reach the end of the road in one piece. I nod, pointing to my iPhone in the storage compartment beside me. While Kate's Mini has a touchscreen display with a built-in satnav, and as much as she relies on it, I do not need a robotic voice directing me on a journey to the Peaks that I've done more times than I can count.

As we head down Euston Road, I hear Kate tut at her phone, her thumbs typing at warp speed.

'You're not still working, are you?' I ask, as we pull up behind a line of traffic. 'I thought we agreed to take Christmas off?'

'We did,' she replies, not lifting her gaze. 'I just need to reply to a couple of emails and then I'll be finished . . . and maybe one phone call, but I can do that at services when we stop.'

I sigh and turn on the radio, knowing that a couple of emails means we're pretty much going to spend the journey in silence, while she batters through her inbox. At least the car is beginning to warm up again.

'Remember you still have a chance to win ten thousand pounds for Christmas here at Heart FM where we play the biggest hits all day every day.'

'God, remember this?' I exclaim, as 'Step into Christmas' begins to play. In year 11, Hope Valley High School held a

Christmas hoedown (for reasons no one fully understood) and Kate and I were thrown together as partners. For two weeks beforehand, instead of PE, the teachers made us learn several cringe-inducing line dances and it was truly one of the most excruciating fortnights of my life. However, this song reminds me of more than just the awkwardness of youth (and the fact that I can still do a mean grapevine); it reminds me of the first time I asked Kate out. In the middle of the gym hall, me wearing a pair of second-hand cowboy boots and ill-fitting jeans, and she still said yes.

My mental lasso dancing is rudely interrupted when Kate sighs loudly and switches off the radio. 'I can't concentrate with that bloody song playing.'

'Jeez, grumpy are we, Ebeneezer?' I reply, somewhat hurt that she doesn't remember the significance of this Christmas masterpiece. 'Just trying to get us into the Christmas spirit.'

'Sorry,' she replies. 'I'm just not in the mood for festive songs yet . . . and I swear, if you play that version of Slade's "Merry Xmas Everybody" where that Scottish guy just repeats the "hanging up your stocking" line over and over for the entire song, I will kill you.'

'But it's really funny . . .' I begin, letting my words trail off when I realise she's not even listening, her thumbs continuing to tap at speed. I stare straight ahead in silence, determined to get her to unwind, even if she does indeed kill me. Never mind, I think. In a few hours we'll be at my parents' house, drinking mulled wine and—

'Wait, why are you going this way?' she asks, momentarily looking away from her phone.

'What do you mean?' I ask, confused by the deep frown lines which have now taken over her forehead. 'This is the way we always go.'

She points to the road ahead. 'It's completely gridlocked, Ed. Which GPS are you using? We should be able to get around this, surely. I mean, is it even switched on? I haven't heard any voice commands.'

'Um, I must have it on mute or something. I'll sort it when we stop.'

Bugger. I was hoping to avoid this. Before I can say anything else, Kate grabs my phone and turns on the screen.

'Are you kidding me, Ed?' she says, scrolling through my open tabs. 'You have three map apps on this phone, and you haven't even opened one of them!'

'I don't need to,' I inform her. 'I know this journey like the back of my hand.'

'Does the back of your hand also give you real-time traffic updates?' she replies, tossing my phone into the cupholder. 'We could have avoided all this if you'd just used Waze . . . or Google Maps. Christ, even Apple maps is better than nothing!'

'It wouldn't have mattered, anyway,' I insist, driving

approximately three feet forwards. 'No GPS is going to magically part the fucking traffic like Moses.'

'It's two days before Christmas. Everyone's heading out of London. You should have gone via the M40. You don't need a satnav to tell you that.'

'I don't need a satnav to tell me anything, Kate!' I exclaim, my festive glow beginning to dampen. 'I could do this journey with my eyes closed.'

'Of course, you could – we're not bloody moving!'

'Look, I'm sorry you've had a shitty day, but don't take it out on me. If you'd actually been on time we might have—'

She drops her phone on her lap. 'Well, *excuse* me for taking my job seriously, Ed,' she snipes. 'Heaven forbid someone in this relationship has some ambition.'

'Well, that was uncalled for,' I say, continuing to creep forwards a whole two inches. 'And what the hell do you even mean by that? I'm a teacher – that's hardly unambitious. I don't understand you sometimes.'

'Exactly. How can you possibly understand my situation if you've never cared about being successful?'

'Our definitions of success are obviously very different,' I reply coldly. 'And, for the record, I find it bizarre that you would keep yourself in a job you hate, surrounded by people you dislike, just to earn a bit extra.'

'A bit extra? You mean the bit that pays for most of the rent? That bit?'

'Fucking hell, not everything is about money, Kate!' I

exclaim, tempted to stop the virtually stationary car and get out. 'Yes, you earn more than me but at least I'm happy. You used to be happy, remember?'

'Barely,' she mumbles.

'And once upon a time you had your heart set on Human Rights Law so you could *make a difference*. All that humanity suddenly vanished when they added an extra zero to your salary, didn't it?'

'Well, I remember when you wanted to perform music, not teach it. You have so much talent in composing, songwriting, singing. But noooo, as usual, anything that requires you to take yourself out of your little bubble isn't worth the effort.'

We sit and seethe in silence. What a fucking start to Christmas this is. I turn on my Apple music and click on the playlist I've spent ages compiling for the journey – *Merry Bopmas*. As the harmonium kicks in and the bassline descends, I instantly regret making the first track *that version of Slade's 'Merry Xmas Everybody' where that Scottish guy just repeats the 'hanging-up-your-stocking' line over and over.*

'Fucking hell, Ed are you just trying to piss me off?'

I quickly skip it. 'No, I'm not, Kate. I put it on there before I knew you'd be homicidal for the entire journey. I don't get it. You laughed at that song the first time you heard it. What the hell happened?'

She throws her hands in the air. 'I laughed at SpongeBob

SquarePants as a kid. Does that mean I still have to laugh at it now? People change, Ed.'

'Well, I haven't changed,' I reply, omitting the fact that I still laugh at SpongeBob. 'I'm still the same person you met fifteen years ago.'

'Exactly!' she yells. 'Maybe that's the problem. People are supposed to change. We are supposed to evolve.'

'So I'm the problem?' I say, laughing in disbelief. 'Wow. OK. Nothing to do with your unwillingness to actually put some effort into this relationship.'

'What, because I don't want to be married with five kids by the time I'm thirty?' she asks. 'I know you were an only child, Ed, but that doesn't mean my womb is going to give you a basketball team to make up for it.'

'Oh, silly me,' I reply. 'How stupid of me to assume that we were planning for the future like a normal couple. You know, building a life together and—'

'You're building a life that I don't want!'

My blood finally boils. 'Oh, fuck you.'

I see her lip tremble, but she stares straight ahead. 'I think we should take a break. This isn't working anymore.'

I nod. 'At last, something we agree on.'

As she turns to face me, the traffic finally starts to move.

Kate

In 2014, singer Tara Mitchell left the hugely successful girl group Hype to start a family with her famous premiership footballer husband, Andrew Brown. Two children, a TV panel chat show, countless magazine deals and a very public affair later, Tara Mitchell-Brown opted to divorce Andrew and take advantage of our firm's notoriously ruthless reputation in order to, and I quote, 'take the cheating, lying wazzock for everything he's got'.

While managing partner, Harriet Parish, was delighted to have Tara (and her forthcoming settlement) as a client, she was less delighted to be dealing directly with someone with a strong Geordie accent who openly supports the Labour Party.

'She's from your neck of the woods, Kate – I'm sure you'll be able to offer her excellent representation. I think Julian is perhaps a little too public school for this one. They wouldn't click. You've made quite a name for yourself, dealing with these reality-TV-personality types – keep it up.'

About a year after I joined the family law department at Parish Scott Taylor, I began to realise that I wasn't hired solely on merit. A department which normally represented high-ranking politicians, bankers and CEOs quickly understood that the rise in popularity of influencers, WAGS, content creators and social media stars, was a highly lucrative market to tap into. Even five minutes of fame could be turned into a brand, making millions from deals, endorsements, merchandise and public appearances. They were young, rich and (fortunately for our firm) tended to get married rather impulsively. But, unlike the majority of our clients, they were, well . . . normal people. Normal people who didn't own Fortune 500 companies, or sit on the front benches in parliament, or continue to give themselves fat bonuses at the end of a poor financial year. They were relatable. Likeable. They had regional accents and a state-school education and were smart enough not to squander an opportunity, working their backsides off to have a better life. Which is why I was hired. These people were me.

I still get drafted in to work on the occasional megabucks marriage dissolution, where the list of assets reads like a Harrods brochure, but over the past six months, I've dealt with a YouTube creator with over 26 million followers, a reality-TV star with a fitness empire and (my favourite) a *MasterChef* contestant with a lucrative TV and book deal, who divorced a property tycoon, then anonymously donated her settlement to a children's hospital because she was determined that *something good should come out of this shitshow*.

Ed just doesn't get it. He doesn't understand why I work so hard in a job which makes me unhappy. Why I chose this over human rights – undoubtedly, a far more noble pursuit. I tell him that I took this job in family law because my mother was left with nothing after my father divorced her. Not that he had much, but nothing was in her name. Not even her car which he loaded up with her things and took. I tell him I work hard to make sure everyone is treated fairly, especially the children, and while this is true, it isn't the whole story. I do have another motive but it's one which I'm ashamed to admit, even though I feel it in my bones. I choose to work in this environment because I'm surrounded by people who haven't settled for a mediocre life, and I'm scared to death that I might wake up one day and realise that's exactly what I have.

When we pull up at Welcome Break motorway services, Ed and I haven't spoken for forty minutes. He breaks this silence momentarily to ask if I want anything to eat but I shake my head, the lump in my throat preventing me from saying anything at all.

'See you back here, then,' he mumbles, taking the keys out of the ignition.

I grab my bag and make my way to the bathrooms, desperately trying to get into a cubicle before I begin to cry.

I use the toilet, wash my hands, then take a moment to compose myself, hoping my face isn't actually as red as the fluorescent lighting in here suggests. Christ, I look a mess. *Nothing like a mirror in a public bathroom to make you feel worse about yourself*, I think, trying to flatten the crown of flyaway hairs which has formed on top of my head. Jesus, it looks like someone's rubbed my head with a balloon.

Normally, this would be the time when I meet up with Ed at the food court and we compete to find the worst sandwich possible, which, given the choice, is actually more difficult than it sounds. Ed won in October with an egg and cheese monstrosity which got hurled out of the car window at 70mph, while I won in June with a prawn baguette which smelled like it was made in 1955. These road trips used to be like a little adventure, a chance to get away from everything and just relax. Be silly. Just be Ed and Kate – the two idiots who met at fourteen and have made each other laugh every day since.

I take a breath and wipe the mascara from under my eyes before making my way into the food court. I feel too upset to eat but I'll grab some water for the car. I could murder a cigarette, but he'd only spend the rest of the journey moaning about the smell.

I return to the car where Ed is already back in the driver's seat. I usually drive the second half of the journey, but I don't mention it. He still looks angry and at this point, it really doesn't matter. I slip into the passenger seat and close the door.

'Shall we just head home, then?' he snarls. 'Cos, there's no way I'm breaking this news to my parents at Christmas. I'd rather say we broke down or died or something.'

Shit. My family. They are not going to take this well either. They all love Ed. Probably more than I do, especially my little brother, Tom. He adores him.

'Well, we can't not go,' I reply. 'They're expecting us. My mum has made you that avocado vegetarian crap you like.'

'So now being vegetarian is a problem?' he responds. 'At least I care about my diet. I'm not the one who couldn't button their jeans at the weekend.'

I gasp. 'Are you calling me fat?'

He shrugs. 'Just stating a fact. My waist is the same size it's been since I was fifteen.'

'Not the only part of you that didn't grow then . . .'

'Mature, Kate,' he responds. 'Very mature.'

'Well don't call me fat, avocado boy.'

We sit again in silence, staring out of opposite windows.

'Look, we're halfway there,' I finally say, realising that we can't just sit forever in a service station. 'They're expecting us. Let's just go, smile and deal with this mess when we get home.'

He frowns. 'Are you serious? You expect me to act like none of this just happened? You're unreal.'

'What's the alternative? Just not show up and ruin everyone's fun?'

'Wouldn't be the first time . . .'

I give a frustrated shriek, which makes him jump. 'Really? You're bringing *that* up. I was in court, Ed! We got held up. They don't tend to let you postpone because you have dinner plans.'

'It was my birthday!'

'Oh, grow up.'

He folds his arms and continues to look out of the window while I consider hitching a ride on the HGV that's just pulled in.

'Look, your parents are expecting us,' I say again, firmly. I'm pretty sure we can be adult enough to get through this. OK?'

'Fine.' He sits sulking for a few more seconds before starting the car. 'Can't believe you made a joke about my knob,' he mumbles as we drive away.

Three rather stressful hours later, we approach a familiar sign on the road ahead. *Welcome to Castleton.* It doesn't matter how often I make this journey, I still feel a sense of calm the moment we enter the village – like stepping into the wardrobe and finding that behind it exists a land without Pret a Manger and pollution. The old, pale-bricked houses with their little stone-walled gardens look as charming at night as they do during the day but especially so at Christmas. Fairy lights dressing bare trees line the road and the B&Bs with 'No Vacancy' signs let me know that the pubs will be busy with hikers and backpackers, but this is nothing new. People flock here all year round and I especially like it when they bring their dogs. I always wanted a dog but my mum said she had enough on her plate without vet bills and chewed furniture, so she got me a goldfish instead.

Castleton is the place where I grew up and Ed moved to when he was fourteen, and while it's hardly the most exciting village in the world, we made the most of it. With a population of only 600, we were forced to make our own fun, often meeting up with classmates from neighbouring villages who were just as desperate to leave as we were. I often wonder if Ed and I would have been so close if we'd grown up in a city or attended a high school with more than three hundred pupils.

My mum and I moved to Hope twelve years ago when she married my stepdad, Gary, a gentle man with a penchant for soda bread and bird watching – a far cry from my biological dad, Brian, whose proclivities were limited to heavy drinking, arse scratching and attempted life ruining. Thankfully, Hope is only a mile and a half down the road from Castleton, so Ed and I were unaffected, but I was always sad to leave my first home. While it might not have held great memories for Mum, it did for me.

Even at one-thirty in the morning, we see hikers

making their way into the village, night-walk headlamps still attached to their woolly hats. However, as we drive further into the village, my stomach knots as we pass the Blue John Craft Shop, which has been here longer than I have. It's the only place in the world where you can mine Blue John stone and Ed bought me a necklace from there for my eighteenth birthday, just before we left Castleton separately for uni. A small love heart with a purple blue stone on a silver chain. I still think it's the most beautiful gift I've ever received.

A couple of minutes later we pull up outside Ed's parents' home – a detached Victorian house which they've spent the past decade renovating. As usual, it looks like they've gone all out for Christmas; flashing fairy lights on the front hedges, spray snow on the windows and a beautiful wreath on the door, which I know will smell of cinnamon and spiced orange room spray. It always does.

Ed turns off the engine, and we sit for a moment, neither of us ready to face the next few days. Before long, the curtains twitch and I see Yvonne, Ed's mum, waving frantically.

'Let's get this over with,' he mutters, waving back. 'I thought they'd already be in bed. Fuck, she's wearing an elf jumper.'

I wave too, watching Chris, Ed's dad, bound down the path. For a seventy-year-old, he's certainly sprightly. He's wearing the same jumper as Yvonne, only the elf's face is tightly stretched over his stomach, dragging it out of shape. As much as I want to laugh, I'm too drained.

'You're here!' Chris announces, gleefully, as we exit the car. 'Here, give me those bags, and let's get you in. Your mother's been worried.'

'Didn't you get Kate's text?' Ed asks, handing the first bag to his dad.

Chris shakes his head. 'Your mother got a new phone. I'm not even sure she knows how to turn it on. You know what us oldies are like.'

Ed was a 'late' baby, or as Yvonne likes to say *her little miracle,* as she fell pregnant in her forties, which always seemed so old to me growing up; my mum and dad had me when they were sixteen.

Understandably, they absolutely dote on Ed but constantly mention that they wish they'd had a bigger family. Given their age, I understand why Ed wants to give them a grandchild but I'm just not ready. I'm not sure I'll ever be.

'She was running late as usual and we hit traffic,' I hear Ed remark as I walk around to the boot and take out a bag of presents.

'Well, he didn't use GPS,' I say, in a passive-aggressive, sing-song tone, intentionally standing on his toe as I lean in to hug Chris. 'You know what he's like. Merry Christmas, Chris.'

'Come on you lot, you'll freeze to death out there,'

Yvonne yells from the front door, not caring that it's almost 2am and her neighbours are asleep.

I see Ed plaster a smile on his face as he walks up the path to greet his mum, who hugs him like she didn't just see him in October. I walk behind, trying not to skid on the path which has begun to freeze over.

'Bitter out, isn't it, my love?' Yvonne says in a soft east London accent. 'You look gorgeous as usual, doesn't she Chris?'

'She does,' he confirms, as Yvonne squeezes the life out of me. Even though Chris is also from east London, he went to boarding school where, apparently, they *knocked the cockney out of him*, so his accent is far more generic. Ed's accent is soft like his mum's and far nicer than my Derbyshire drawl, though he'd disagree.

We shuffle through the entrance hall and place the bags at the top of the basement stairs, which lead to Ed's old room, though they've taken down all of his Oasis posters, added a small en-suite and undoubtedly fumigated it to remove the odour of teenage boy.

'Now, you'll have a glass of something, won't you?' Yvonne asks, pulling me into the living room. 'I've got some of that Christmas flavoured Baileys in and mince pies from Sal at the market. You remember Sal, yeah?'

'Sal, of course,' I reply, having no clue who she's talking about. 'But I'm exhausted, Yvonne. I might just head to bed and then we can do this properly tomorrow?'

Ed appears behind me and flops down on to the couch. 'I'll have one with you, Mum,' he says, kicking off his shoes. 'Kate's had a long day.'

'You sure, love?' she asks.

I nod. 'Sorry – I wouldn't be much company. But I'll see you all in the morn . . . well, a few hours!'

This is the point where Ed would normally tell me he'll be down soon, but he doesn't say a word. I give Yvonne a kiss on the cheek and trudge down to the basement.

'Wow, you've really spruced this room up!' I say, admiring the new décor. 'Ed never said.' This doesn't surprise me, though. I once painted our white kitchen lemon while he was away chaperoning a school trip for three days and it took him a week to notice.

'Yeah,' Chris replies. 'We got Phil Horne in to do it. Yvonne was fed up with the green.'

It's beautiful. The dark green walls are gone, replaced with a champagne-coloured wallpaper and new floor. It looks like a hotel suite. They've even placed a little gold Christmas tree in the corner of the room.

Chris pushes my case against the wall before straightening up with a groan.

'Oh, I could have done that,' I tell him. 'Don't do yourself a mischief running about after us.'

'Nonsense,' he replies. 'It's no bother. You not having a nightcap? Your mum's been going on about that Baileys all week.'

Your mum. He's been doing this for a couple of years now and I never correct him. Neither does Ed. We figured it's either his age or he simply sees me as his daughter-in-law, given that I've been dating Ed for so long. I know Ed secretly likes it; to him, it's one step further in his quest to wife me. I smile and tell him I'll try the Baileys tomorrow, but I'm just absolutely beat.

'OK, love, sleep well,' he replies, turning on the bedside lamp. 'I'll send the boy down soon, though you'll probably be glad of five minutes to yourself.'

His eyes sparkle, the way Ed's do. I mean, Ed's always been like his dad, but I see it more than ever tonight. The same wide brown eyes, the way they both stand with their hands in their pockets when they feel a tad awkward, but most of all, the way I feel completely at home whenever I'm around them, regardless of where we are, though I've lost that with Ed recently. These days we just seem to pass like ships in the night . . . actually, more like stray cats in the night, occasionally mating and hissing at each other as we go.

Chris closes the door behind him as I kick off my shoes, unreasonably miffed that they've replaced the carpet in here with wooden flooring, but I'm grateful to have a minute alone. I half-heartedly wash my face and brush my teeth before climbing into bed. New mattress. New pillows which appear to be filled with some kind of memory-foam cement. I punch them into submission and lie back, closing my eyes and hoping that I'm asleep before Ed comes in. But as tired as I am, I couldn't be less relaxed if I tried. Being here normally fills me with a sense of calm but this time it's different, and it's not the room or the new mattress or the stupidly firm pillows. It's me. It's us. We're different.

Today just seems so surreal but not entirely unsurprising. One of us needed to say something, to finally admit that we weren't happy. But what happens now? I've never broken up with anyone before. Ed's been my only boyfriend for the past fourteen years. He's all I've ever known.

2006

Ed

'Kelly-Anne, take Edward with you to the lunch hall and show him the ropes, will you?'

I watch Kelly-Anne's satsuma-coloured face scowl as she lifts her folder from the desk in front of me, making sure our headteacher Mr Cartwright is out of earshot before tutting loudly.

'Why is it always me?' she mutters. 'Do I look like a feckin' babysitter? Hurry up, then,' she growls at the new kid, beckoning with a badly tanned hand towards the back of the class. 'I want to get a burger before they're all gone.'

The new kid just nods and grabs his backpack, following behind Kelly-Anne like a human puppy who's surprisingly tall for a year 10.

I don't envy anyone having to start a new school, especially one like Hope Valley Comprehensive where, given there's only three hundred students over six year groups, the new-friend pickings here are rather slim. I only have one close friend, Lauren Alexander, but she selfishly decided to get glandular fever and hasn't been in school all week.

I pick up my bag and walk down the stairs to the lunch hall, joining the rest of the ravenous lunch-line zombies, who, like me, weren't smart enough to bring something from home. The only thing worth eating here are the burgers but that queue is almost out the door, so I settle for a ham sandwich which I will add crisps to and live dangerously.

I park myself on a bench at the back of the room, knowing that everyone will fill up the middle benches first and I don't want to get stuck between Kelly-Anne's clique of badly drawn lips and Jason Jessop's sixth-form cronies who look down on anyone who doesn't have a provisional licence yet.

The smell of Thursday's chili fills the halls, making me gag. It smells like a mixture of body odour and arse, though to be fair, half of the boys here smell like that anyway, despite the overuse of Lynx body spray.

I open my sandwich and start placing my cheese and onion crisps neatly on top of the ham, briefly pausing to shoo away some year 7s who attempt to break the golden rule of sitting anywhere except the front benches. They look like little turtles with their backpacks on, shouting at each other in annoying South Park voices. What a day to have working ears. I'm not in the mood for any of this. I'm exhausted, and I just want to be left alone. Maybe if

Mum and Dad hadn't been screaming at each other all bloody night I might have got a good night's—

'I see the food here's no better than my last place.'

My eyes dart right to the end of the bench and see the new guy suspiciously examining his pasta. I shrug and turn back to my own culinary masterpiece.

'I'm Ed, by the way,' he says. 'I think we're in the same geography class.'

'There is only one geography class for year 10,' I mumble, reading the ingredients on the back of my crisps packet.

'Not much of a talker, then?' he continues. 'Do you at least have a name?'

I turn and scowl. *Look, Ed, my parents are probably getting a divorce, which means I'm going to have to choose whether to live with a drunk or a thirty-one-year-old woman who keeps wearing my clothes. So no, I'm not up for a chit-chat right now . . .* is what I don't say because I haven't told anyone about my folks, not even Lauren. I don't even want to admit it to myself yet. Instead, I just glower, hoping he'll take the hint.

As I crunch up the last of my crisps, and place them in my sandwich, I hear Ed scrunching his own bag of crisps, loudly. I glance over and see him scowling while pouring his crisps on his pasta.

'What are you doing?' I ask.

'Being you,' he replies, 'No . . . wait . . .' He stops and brushes his black hair over his face. 'There we go.'

'Oh, very funny,' I say, wishing my hair actually looked

as cool as his does now. Mine looks like I dried it in a tornado, which, given the weather today, is probably an accurate description.

He scowls again and stabs his crisp pasta with his fork, sighing dramatically. I smirk.

As he eats, I see his face change from a fake frown to something more in line with disgust. 'Bad idea,' he says, putting down his fork.

'Didn't think that through, did you?' I ask, my smirk becoming wider.

He shakes his head and pushes his plate away. 'Worcester Sauce crisps and creamy leek pasta don't mix well. Who'd have thought?'

'People with taste buds?' I respond, inwardly wondering why anyone would choose the leek pasta. 'Oh, and the canteen has just closed. Good luck starving to death.'

He laughs and his face starts to flush. 'Fucked this right up, didn't I?'

'Well, maybe spend less time making fun of people and—'

'I wasn't making fun of you; not really,' he interrupts. 'It was just my clumsy way of trying to talk to you. Sorry. I haven't really spoken to anyone today. I'm not normally this weird.'

My heart sinks. I feel like such a bitch and I'm not. Not really. No more than any other fourteen-year-old who has unruly red hair, freckles, and hates her entire life.

'I'm sorry,' I say. 'Just having a shit day.'

'Cos of your hair?'

I laugh so loudly that even the sixth-formers turn around.

'I'm kidding, I'm kidding,' Ed insists, grinning. 'Your hair is awesome. You look like Molly Ringwald. Sorry, she's an actress, I forget that not everyone is a massive nerd like me.'

I feel my own face start to flush. 'I loved *The Breakfast Club*, and *Pretty in Pink*.'

'Me too! I'm kind of an eighties' movie geek, you know, when I'm not ruining lunch and stuff.'

As he smiles, something in me just melts. I hand him the other half of my sandwich.

'Kate,' I tell him. 'My name is Kate.'

DECEMBER 24TH – CHRISTMAS EVE

Ed

'Breakfast in ten minutes! I hope you're both hungry.'

I open one eye and glance at my phone. It's nine-thirty but I didn't get to bed until well after three. I feel a tad hungover. Dad gave me some of his favourite Scotch whisky, which really doesn't affect him too much but has the tendency to knock me on my arse after more than two glasses. Thank god, he got some beers in; there's no way I can drive to Kate's parents' tomorrow feeling like this.

I hear Kate stir beside me – that little morning moan she does when she's far too comfortable to even consider getting up. She turns around and slips her arm through mine, letting it rest on my chest before nuzzling into my neck. She's so warm. So soft. For a second my body wants to respond, but it passes as yesterday's fight floods my brain.

You're building a life that I don't want.

I edge my body towards the side of the bed, moving her arm. 'Probably not the best idea. I'm not in the mood.'

She sniffs and rubs her eyes. 'Mood for what?'

'Forget it,' I reply, now wondering if she'd snuggled into me unintentionally. 'I'm going to get dressed, breakfast is nearly ready.'

'Yeah, fine,' she replies, still half asleep. 'I'll be up in a minute.'

I throw on some jogging trousers and yesterday's jumper, following the smell of bacon and coffee until I reach the dining room. My dad's already seated, wearing his overstretched elf again as Bing Crosby croons through the Bluetooth speakers I gave him last year.

'Happy Christmas Eve, my love!' Mum exclaims, placing a toast rack on the table.

'Tea or coffee?'

I swear if Mum hadn't spent all those years teaching piano, she'd have run a bed and breakfast. Every time I visit, she lays the table like I'm a paying guest, with miniature pots of jam and marmalade, individual butter portions, three different juices, cereal, pastries and, of course, her famous fry-up. Saying that, if she hadn't taught piano, I'd probably never have got into music; but I'd know how to cook sausages without them exploding.

'Tea, thanks,' I reply, grabbing some toast and hoping it will soak up the remnants of last night's booze. 'And yes, Happy Christmas Eve. But this music . . . don't we have anything a little less . . .'

'Relaxing?' she replies, her eyes narrowing. 'Timeless?'

'I was going for snooze-inducing,' I say, smiling. 'Maybe something a bit peppier to get into the festive mood?'

'It's ten in the morning, Eddie. I'll whack on some Boney M later.'

Oh god, here it comes.

'Do you remember when you were little, and you used to dance to "Mary's Boy Child" in your Santa pyjamas? Aw, you were ever so sweet.'

Every year I'm reminded of this. Every bloody year.

'How could I forget?' I reply. 'Pretty sure you videotaped it. Um, how's that tea coming along?'

'I'll just bring the pot,' she informs me. 'Oh and I got those plant-based, meat-free thingamabobs for you. We did a shop at the big Waitrose.'

'I'll never understand how they can make a sausage from a plant,' dad interjects, rubbing his glasses on the elf's face.

'You'd be surprised what they can do these days,' I inform him, not wanting to get into the whole plant-vs-pig debate yet again. Even in my teens, he was utterly confused as to why anyone would willingly give up meat. *You should be eating nose to tail, son. You need that protein. We have incisors for a reason.*

'Not wearing your Elf jumper today, Mum?' I ask, steering the conversation away from grass burgers or whatever my dad is currently rambling about.

'No, love,' she shouts from the kitchen. 'It's in the wash.

Spilled me bloody Advocaat down it, didn't I? I do love a fluffy duck, though.'

Hearing this said in a cockney accent, it's very hard not to think it's rhyming slang for something more vulgar than a harmless cocktail.

'Sorry, everyone. I couldn't drag myself out of bed.'

I turn to see Kate sheepishly hovering at the door. She's wearing her jeans and the long, black baggy jumper she wears when she's feeling bloated or just unhappy with her body. My heart sinks. Fuck – that comment I made yesterday. It was mean and completely unnecessary.

'There's my favourite daughter-in-law!' Mum exclaims, over the top of a huge tray of dead animal flesh. 'Don't stand on ceremony, lovely, sit down.'

'I told you to let me carry that, Yvonne,' Dad says but she shoos him away, placing it in the centre of the table.

Kate smiles and pulls out the chair beside me. 'Smells amazing,' she praises, picking up a cup. 'And you look wonderful, Yvonne. Love that colour on you. Is that jade?'

'Emerald green,' my mum replies, as she heads to the kitchen. 'John Lewis sale. Glad *someone* noticed.'

My dad and I glance at each other in shame. He follows Mum into the kitchen and returns with my plate, assuring me that it wasn't cooked with the 'real food'.

'Dig in, everyone,' Mum instructs, passing the ketchup to Dad.

I grab some more toast and fold it around some vegan

bacon and brown sauce, immediately feeling more human.

As I see Kate spear a couple of sausages and some mushrooms, it occurs to me that it's been a long time since I've seen her eat breakfast. She's usually leaving for work, while I'm getting ready, then she'll grab something from Pret or Starbucks on the way in; though she'll always make sure to fill up the teapot for me before she leaves.

'Now after breakfast, I'm stealing this one for a girlie chat,' Mum announces, much to Kate's surprise.

'Oh, well, I've actually got a couple of things I need to—'

'Nothing that can't wait, I'm sure,' I say, through gritted teeth. She can't seriously be thinking about working today. She smiles at me, but I can tell she's plotting my demise. Something painful if the kick to my shin is any indication.

'We'll have a nice walk,' Mum continues. 'Maybe pop into the Outdoor Shop, I could use some new gloves for this evening – it's to be a cold one.'

'This evening?' I ask, through a mouthful of beans. 'You going out?'

'We all are,' Mum replies. 'Carol concert, up the Devil's Arse. Ring any bells? I mean we only do it every year, Ed.'

'Oh yeah,' I say. 'Must have slipped my mind.'

'And I was going to wait till later, but since we're on the subject . . .' She reaches to the side of the table and lifts two parcels, wrapped in shiny red paper. 'You'll be needing these.'

Mine feels squishy. It feels like a jumper.

'What have you done, Mum?' I ask, tentatively removing the paper, while Kate tears at hers. 'Please tell me these aren't—'

'Matching Christmas jumpers.'

I turn towards Kate's voice and see her holding up a Rudolph jumper. The same one I've just unwrapped.

Mum almost bursts with delight and screeches while Dad chuckles and slaps me on the back. 'We've all got them. If you press the nose, it lights up. Hilarious!'

If Kate *is* going to kill me, now would be the perfect time.

Kate

'Did you know that you can only mine Blue John here in the whole of the UK?' Yvonne asks as we stroll through the village. 'That always amazes me.'

'Hmm,' I reply. 'Isn't that something.'

Sometimes I think that Yvonne forgets I grew up here. She often regales me with facts about Castleton that I learned in primary school, long before she even moved here. It's like me taking her round the East End of London and asking her if she's heard of Jack the Ripper.

I feel my phone vibrate in my pocket and take a quick peek while Yvonne continues to tell me shit I already know. It's my client, Tara – the one I said I'd call an hour ago before Ed decided that a walk with his mother was more important than my job. Her one missed call has now morphed into three unread messages and I feel my stress levels starting to rise again. I need to deal with this, so I can get on with enjoying this bloody holiday.

'Yvonne, let me buy you a coffee,' I suggest, spotting

a café across the road. 'I could use something to warm me up.'

Yvonne agrees, before telling me that the café was once owned by William the Conqueror or something but I'm not listening. I need a toilet cubicle and five minutes to reply to Tara.

'Back in a sec,' I tell her as she sits at a table near the window. 'Order anything you'd like,' but now Yvonne's not listening, as a woman and her Pomeranian have just walked in, and the entire café is asking if he's a good boy.

I'm forced to wait for a cubicle, enduring sounds that I'd rather forget, until one becomes free. I lock the door and take out my phone.

> Kate, I emailed u but ur out of office is on. He's taken me bloody foot spa (u know the good one with the magnets and the infrared lights) and given it to that bint! I've just seen an Instagram post with her crusty size 8s crammed in there.

Seriously? This is what she's been so desperate to talk to me about? A foot spa? Of course, I understand that the problem here runs deeper than the foot spa, but I'm now busy trying to come up with a response that doesn't start with *ARE YOU* and end with *KIDDING ME?*

> Hi Tara, sorry, I'm away for a few days for Christmas (phone signal is poor here) but I'm sure we can sort this out on my return and get your foot spa back for you. Best, Kate.

I've barely even had time to wash my hands before she replies.

Well, I don't want it back, not after she's been ankle deep in it. Just add the value to the settlement. Two grand should do it. It was an irreplaceable gift from my grandmother.

According to Tara's autobiography, *Tara Tells All*, her grandmother died in the late seventies and left behind nothing but a five-pound Premium Bond and a signed photo of Sean Connery. And besides, the foot spa in question was only released last year, so I'm calling bullshit. However, I'll help her come up with a more believable sad story, when I get back to London.

Yvonne has ordered me a latte and a vanilla cupcake, which is now being licked half to death by the Pomeranian while his owner chats to Yvonne. I sit down and inspect my latte for dog hair.

'Just as well I'm on a diet,' I say to the dog, pushing my plate closer to him.

'Oh dear!' his owner exclaims. 'I'm so sorry, I didn't even notice.'

'Violet runs the new holiday cottages,' Yvonne informs me. 'Luther has become quite the local celebrity.'

I smile. 'His name is Luther?' I lean over and pet his head. 'It absolutely suits him, handsome devil that he is.'

'You must let me replace the cake,' Violet insists. 'I'm embarrassed. He's normally so well behaved.'

She won't take no for an answer and soon I'm enjoying a Danish pastry as Luther scoffed the last cupcake.

'You're good with dogs,' Yvonne tells me as we watch Violet and Luther leave the café. 'Just think how wonderful you'll be with children.'

I nearly choke on my pastry. 'Um, I'm no expert but I'm pretty certain that children and dogs are not the same.'

She sips her tea and chuckles. 'I meant the patience and love you give them. You'll be a great mum. You're very caring and efficient. And you know . . . tick, tock, tick, tock . . .'

I smile weakly and go back to my Danish. I knew this would happen. The closer I get to thirty, the more Yvonne keeps bringing up my fucking ticking time bomb of a biological clock.

We walk over to the clothing store, a quirky-looking sand-coloured building which always smells like a mixture of pine air freshener and new shoes. This store has everything for those who love the great outdoors. For everyone from hillwalkers, to climbers, casual strollers and camping fans, this is the place to buy something you'll never use and hang on to it for the next two decades, 'just in case' – like that seventy-two-piece Swiss army knife my dad insisted he needed, and which still sits unused in a drawer to this day.

Yvonne picks out some new, ridiculously overpriced sheepskin gloves, while I grab a black scarf, cursing myself for leaving my perfectly good one at work. I'll need it for tonight, though. It's like the Arctic inside the caves during winter.

'Now would you look at these,' Yvonne says, holding up something pink and fluffy. I lean over and take a closer look before pursing my lips. Baby mittens. 'Hmm,' I reply. 'They look . . . warm.'

'I remember when Eddie was this size. All pink cheeks and fat baby ankles. Did I ever tell you about—'

I switch off and run automatic baby-Eddie-story-nodding mode, but I'm on the verge of tying my own tubes with the climbing rope on display near the cash desk. I'm not sure how much more of this I can take, not with everything else that's going on. The stress of pretending everything is normal between Ed and me is more than I bargained for; however, I'm glad I won't have to be the one to break it to Yvonne.

Half an hour later, we arrive home. I mumble something about having a headache, so I have an excuse to be alone and avoid afternoon tea. We still have a few hours before the Christmas Eve carolling begins – something I normally enjoy (apart from the sound of my own voice breaking rock formations). But tonight I'm dreading it. I just want to go home.

Ed

As we walk along the path leading to the Peak Cavern (also known as the Devil's Arse, due to the farting sound emitted when the cave floods and the water drains), I can hear the band playing jaunty festive music from inside the cave. It reminds me of playing clarinet in the school band and feeling miffed that the teacher wouldn't let me play guitar or piano, which, as a teenager, I felt were far cooler instruments to show off with in front of my peers. No fifteen-year-old wants to hear 'Off to blow yer instrument?' or 'Get yer lips round it, veggie boy!' while they're playing a solo in 'The Lion Sleeps Tonight'. Bully boy, Mark Castle, got detention for a month but told everyone it was totally worth it as I was a poncy, muso. Ironically, years later, his wife would leave him for a session musician who plays the trumpet.

My mum's already humming away to 'The Snow Waltz', her newly gloved hands conducting as we all file inside the cave while my dad unzips his coat, determined to show off his jumper to anyone with eyes. Kate's been quiet since she got back from her walk with Mum, but I'm not pussyfooting around her anymore. If she wants to spend the next few days sulking, that's up to her, but for our family's sake, I hope she doesn't make everyone as uncomfortable as she obviously feels.

The rough, cracked walls of the cave glow under brightly lit Christmas trees and candle decorations which make the exceptionally cold cave appear cosy. It isn't, though. Right now, I'd wear ten stupid Christmas jumpers just to feel anything close to warm.

Most of the seats at the front are already filled but we find four at the side: Mum and Dad in front, with Kate and me behind. Within thirty seconds she's pulled out her phone and started typing.

'Oh, relax,' she says, shaking her head. 'I'm just replying to my mum.'

'I didn't say anything.'

'You didn't have to,' she replies, still typing. 'I can sense that fucking scowl a mile away.'

'Well, maybe if you weren't always on your bloody phone, I wouldn't need to.'

'Maybe if you weren't always on my bloody case, I'd—'

'Sherbet lemon?'

Mum holds out a little paper bag, filled with sweets. I decline but Kate takes one and thanks her. And before we can continue our argument, the band starts playing

'The Twelve Days of Christmas'. The crowd laughs as the local primary-school children stand at the front with large cards depicting what happens on each day. I can't help but chuckle because the partridge looks like a winged gerbil, but Kate remains stony-faced. I get the feeling that if she were to leave, the temperature in the place might rise by at least ten degrees.

By the time we get to 'Silent Night', my mum has leaned into my dad, and I can hear them singing softly. Normally, Kate and I would be doing the same, but we'd be trying to make each other laugh by hitting the wrong notes or singing in weird voices. This year, though, she's practically sitting on the lap of the woman beside her, in order to be nowhere near me. I want to grab her and ask her how we can make this better, how we can have what my parents have, but I already know the answer. My parents have this because they want the same things; and we can't make this better because we don't.

After a rousing rendition of 'We Wish You a Merry Christmas', everyone piles out and heads back down to the village where food stalls have been set up to tempt hungry carollers.

'I fancy a pie,' Dad announces. 'Anyone else?'

'I'll take some chips,' I reply. 'Kate, you want anything?'

'Pie, definitely,' she answers. 'You need a hand, Chris?'

He shakes his head. 'I'll be fine, dear. Yvonne, do you want any—'

'Sausage roll,' she replies, before he can even finish. 'I'm starving.'

The Christmas tradition of ordering decidedly suspicious-looking meat pies from a van after carolling is one that we've maintained for as long as I can remember. My last one was around 2001, before I became vegetarian and I'd be lying if I said I don't miss it just a little bit.

'Ed?'

I turn in the direction of my name, my eyes scanning the crowd of bobble hats and winter coats until they fix upon a familiar face. It's one I haven't seen since university.

'Carly Richardson? Holy shit. I don't believe it!'

Carly gives a little squeal, and she skips towards me, throwing her arms around my neck.

'I knew that was you!' she chirps, squeezing me. 'I'd recognise that hair anywhere!'

I first met Carly when I was sixteen and my mum signed me up for a three-week music camp in Cheshire. We both played clarinet, though she was far more skilled, and she took pity on me, giving me tips with my breathing.

'Mum, look who it is!'

'How are you, Mrs Morrison?' Carly says, before waving at my dad who's walking back with a meat pie. 'You're all looking so well.'

'You haven't changed a bit, lovely,' Mum says. 'Gosh, how long's it been?'

Carly and I look at each other and laugh. 'Six years,' she replies. 'Or is it seven? God, I feel so old!'

'So, what are you doing now?' I ask. 'Still with the English Chamber Orchestra?'

'No,' she replies. 'I actually just accepted a position in Berlin. I leave after New Year.'

'Ah,' I reply. *Die Welt sehen*? Quite right.'

She laughs. '*Ja, so ähnlich.*'

I see Carly glance at Kate, then hold out her hand. 'So sorry, I've just ambushed you all. I don't think we've met. I'm Carly.'

'Kate,' she replies, her eyes widening a little.

'Oh, wow!' she exclaims. 'I've heard so much about you. So happy to finally meet you.'

'Likewise,' Kate replies, smoothing down her hair. She always does that when she's nervous. 'What brings you to Castleford?'

'My sister Bethan's playing in the band,' Carly says, pointing to the blonde woman I recognise as first euphonium. 'I'm staying with her for Christmas, thought this might be a giggle.'

'Hello, stranger!' Dad exclaims, his arms full of individual pies and chips. 'Fancy seeing you here.'

'I like to get around, Mr M.,' she replies, going in for a hug. 'Oh, I think I squashed something. What've you bought? They smell brilliant.'

Dad gestures towards the Peak Pie van. 'Can I get you something?'

'Aww, no, but thank you, I'm just leaving. So happy I got to see you all!'

'Really great to see you, too,' I say, hugging her again. 'Keep in touch, it's been too long!'

'I will. Promise! Bye, everyone.'

As she walks off, Mum gives Dad a quick slap on the arm. 'Jesus, Chris, you nearly got pie all over her lovely coat.'

We arrive home and I kick off my boots, ready to have a few drinks by the fire, maybe watch some cheesy Christmas film before bed. Mum finally gets to open the Baileys and furnishes everyone with a glass whether they want it or not. Dad's decided he's still hungry and puts out some crisps, pâté, crackers, chocolate and an assortment of cheese. Finally, the mystery of the expanded gut is solved.

'Wasn't it nice to see Carly?' Mum says, slipping on her furry slippers. 'Lovely girl. She always reminds me of Goldie Hawn, you know . . . so pretty and petite and bubbly.'

I hear Kate sigh before grabbing a fistful of cheese puffs.

We browse through some films before deciding on *Love, Actually* – because who doesn't love to see simulated sex scenes with Martin Freeman in front of their parents, but it's Mum's favourite film.

'Aww, doesn't she look gorgeous,' Mum declares as Keira Knightley appears in her wedding dress. 'I do love a good wedding.'

Kate catches my eye and we both know what's coming.

'You'd suit that dress, Kate; you'd fill it better on top,

anyway. Though I always pictured you in something more traditional. Less fussy.'

'I can't say I've ever thought about it,' Kate replies, glancing down at her own boobs. 'But good to know.'

'You've never thought about what dress you'd wear on your wedding day?' Mum exclaims. 'Blimey, I think I had mine picked out by the time I could talk.'

Mum's knocking back the Baileys' like it's a milkshake and Kate's looking irritated. I'm starting to feel a little nervous.

'I guess some women just aren't built that way,' Kate responds, shrugging. 'It's not the be all and end all.'

'Can we change the subject?' I ask. 'Look, Mum – there's that blonde girl you like from *Gavin and Stacey*.'

'I do like her,' Mum remarks. 'Beautiful Welsh accent, just like Carly. Don't you just love the way—'

'Oh, for god's sake,' I hear Kate mumble and I shoot her a warning look. She rolls her eyes and goes back to the film but an hour, two fluffy ducks and the sight of kids dressed up for the nativity is all it takes for Mum to finally break Kate.

'They're so precious at that age, aren't they Chris?' she says welling up. 'When you two lovebirds finally settle down, you'll have all this to—'

'Yvonne, with all due respect, please change the subject,' Kate snaps. 'It's been babies and marriage since I got here and honestly, if I've learned anything in my line of work it's that marriage is an outdated institution which people are kicking and screaming to get out of, and the poor kids get stuck in the middle. Quite frankly, it's not something I aspire to. My life is difficult enough. Shit!'

She gets up, picks up her stocking and pins it beside the fireplace before pausing. 'I'm sorry,' she says quietly. 'It's just that . . .'

'What, dear?' Dad asks, while Mum just looks stunned. I pray to every god ever invented that she doesn't drop an atom bomb on Christmas Eve. Kate looks at me, doing her best to hold back the tears I see brimming. My eyes plead back.

'Nothing,' Kate replies. 'I'm going to take a walk. Get some air.'

As she closes the door behind her, I look at my parents and smile weakly. 'She always has this reaction to Richard Curtis films. I wouldn't worry.'

'You should go with her. It's dark outside.'

'She needs a bit of space, Mum,' I reply, hearing the front door close. 'She'll be fine.'

I turn my attention back to the TV, but can't concentrate. Mum's right, of course. I should go with her. A boyfriend would go with her. Christ, even a friend would, but me? Would she want me to? I don't even know what I am to her anymore.

Kate

Christ on a bike, it's freezing. I wrap my new scarf around my neck, hearing my feet crunch into newly formed ice. It's only 10pm but it's pitch black already, though the Christmas lights in almost every home illuminate my way. Not that I have any destination in mind. I just need to walk. I need to smoke.

My first cigarette in two days. It goes straight to my head but I persevere until the nicotine rush becomes familiar again. The pubs are still open, so I'm not entirely alone, nodding politely to punters as I pass, until I reach the old church. I feel like I'm back in high school, finding places to smoke where we wouldn't be seen by anyone we knew. In a place like Castleton, that's a tall order.

I sit on the bench at the entrance, hearing my grandma's voice in my head telling me that if I sit too long on a cold surface, I'll get haemorrhoids. Right now, I'd rather get piles than endure another conversation about weddings or babies or how wonderful and petite and fucking

Welsh Carly is. I stamp my cigarette out under my boot and light another.

I don't think we've met. I'm Carly.

All I could think in that moment was *Really, Ed? This is Carly? This blonde-haired, model-like, German-speaking, appearing-from-fucking-nowhere, Prada-coat-wearing woman is Carly? The friend you talked about but conveniently never introduced me to when I came to visit you in Manchester. No prizes for guessing why.*

I need to talk to Lauren. I need to hear a friendly voice right now. I dial her number and it rings for ages. She's probably in the pub, I think. Or doing something equally fun. Not everyone is spending Christmas Eve alone in front of a cemetery, Kate.

'Where the hell have you been, girl?' Lauren yells down the phone. 'I've been trying to get you for over a week!'

'I'm so sorry, L,' I reply. 'Work has just been . . . ugh, too fucking blah to bore you with. Merry almost Christmas, though.'

'You're a terrible friend,' she states. 'I could have been in jail or on *Love Island* or some shit and you'd never have known.'

'Were you?' I ask.

'Nah, I've just been here, with Dave. He wants to buy a puppy. With me. Like an actual living puppy. Do I look like a bag-it-and-bin-it kind of girl? He's on his own there; no way I'm getting a mutt.'

I laugh. Lauren met Dave last year when her car broke down and he changed her tyre. She's convinced that it was fate that brought them together, rather than the AA.

'How's your work?' I ask. 'Still blow-drying the rich and famous?'

'Dave, can you turn that telly down, I'm trying to have a conversation with a real-life missing person here. Sorry, babe. God – don't even get me started; work has been crazy. I had that one off *Strictly Come Dancing* in last week. I've been doing her hair for four years and she still tells me how to do her fringe.'

Lauren's mum was horrified when she decided to go to hairdressing college instead of university like me. As if it was somehow less worthy than going down the academic route. She even refused to help her fund it. So Lauren applied to an academy in Durham and flat-shared with me, working every hour god sent when she wasn't training. She then moved to London and never looked back, working for Vidal Sassoon, the BBC and as a freelancer on film sets. The moment A-list celebs started raving about her on Instagram, Lauren was set for life. She now part owns a salon in Kensington with a famous make-up artist and her mum is officially barred.

'Listen, I have some news,' I say tentatively. God, I'm not even sure I want to say it out loud, not even to my best friend of seventeen years.

'Oh god, you're getting married, aren't you?' she

exclaims, 'I knew it. That big, tall drink of water finally wore you down. Well, if I'm doing your hair, I'll need notice. I'm booked up until death.'

'Nooo!' I reply, trying to get a word in while she makes herself chief bridesmaid. 'It's quite the opposite, actually, L. Ed and I . . . well, we're splitting up.'

'Bullshit,' she responds. 'There's no way . . . right? Kate? Kate, are you crying?'

I try to reply but nothing comes out.

'If this is real, sniff once for yes.'

I sniff.

'Oh fuck, Kate,' she replies. 'How? Why? Did he ask you to get a dog, too?'

As I laugh, a huge snot bubble appears. Totally worth it.

'We're just on different paths,' I manage to say. 'He wants the whole kids and marriage thing and I want—'

'A life of debauchery and endless cock?' she replies. 'No, wait. A meaningless existence where you eventually die alone leaving only a legacy of bitterness and regret?'

'Jesus,' I say. 'Way to make a girl feel good.'

'Well, what is it, then?' she presses.

I feel like I've genuinely insulted her. I know she adores Ed but I'm her best mate, not him.

'I'm not even sure,' I reply. 'I just want something more than being a wife and a mother.'

'Hmm,' she replies. 'That's pretty disrespectful to wives and mothers.'

'Oh,' I say. 'I mean, I didn't—'

'Shut up,' she laughs. 'I get it. You don't want to play Suzie Homemaker with a couple of kids under your feet. You want to see the world. Experience life.'

'Exactly!' I reply. 'That's exactly it.'

'Brilliant!' she exclaims. 'Now let me just email every single successful wife and mother on my books. You know, the ones who have homes in Paris, whose kids are so fucking cool and well adjusted, it makes me sick. Who have happy marriages to men that—'

'Fine!' I yell over her. 'I get it, I get it. Fuck, why did I even call you? You don't even like dogs.'

'All I'm saying is don't discount an entire life you've never experienced. If you really don't want marriage and kids, I totally support this. But if it's purely because you think they represent some kind of barrier, preventing you becoming the next Beyoncé of the law world or whatever, then that's just silly.'

'Beyoncé? Really?'

'You know what I mean,' she says, laughing. 'Anyway, I'm off. Enjoy your last Christmas as a spoken-for woman. You'll be shunned by society by the time you get home.'

She hangs up and I just stare at my mobile, unsure whether that actually helped or not.

'You forgot your gloves.'

'Fuck!' I yelp, nearly lifting off my seat. 'You scared the shit out of me.'

Ed grins, though he does his best to conceal it. 'That'll happen around graveyards.' He hands me my gloves and I stuff them into my pocket, along with my phone.

'I thought I lost them at the cavern,' I reply. 'How did you know I'd be here?'

'Wild guess,' he answers, sitting down beside me. 'Maybe because this is where we used to come and smoke.'

'Where I used to smoke,' I correct. 'You just used to have a drag and turn green.'

His mouth smirks but his eyes stay glued to my ciggy. 'Thought you'd given up.'

I shrug. 'Desperate times and all that. And don't go smoke-shaming me. I'm not in the mood.'

He sits back and puts his hands in his pockets. 'Do you remember when we used to sneak into the cemetery during the summer?'

I nod. 'How could I forget? Definitely the weirdest place I've ever been felt up.'

He laughs. 'There'd be little groups of us, all dotted around, hidden by gravestones.'

A wave of nostalgia nearly knocks me off my seat. The smell of the summer-night air, the risk of being caught and the thrill of being sixteen and kissing like your life depends on it. But now here we are, almost fifteen years later and the thrill has gone.

'Carly seems nice,' I say, nonchalantly. 'Like, soopah nice.'

He rolls his eyes at my Welsh accent. 'She is, yeah.'

'But see I'm a little confused – because I distinctly remember you describing her as homely.'

'Did I?'

'Oh yes, you sure did. But unless that home is the fucking Playboy mansion, I'm wondering why.'

'This is why!' He sighs. 'Because of this! This very reaction.' He gestures at me wildly, which would almost be funny if he wasn't implying that I am being unreasonable.

'I think it's a fair question,' I respond, calmly. 'If I spent weeks away from you, shacked up with Tom Hardy, telling you he looks like Boris bloody Johnson, you'd be examining my motives, too.'

'Because you're insecure, Kate,' he tells me. 'I'm sorry but it's true. You hate your hair, your weight, Christ even your freckles, and sometimes it's exhausting. Believe it or not, my intentions were good, I just didn't want it to feed into that bullshit you carry with you.'

'Bollocks,' I respond. 'You kept her quiet because you fancy her and I mean, what's not to fancy?'

'I can't win with you, can I?'

I stub out my cigarette and stand up. 'My arse is numb,' I reply. 'I'm heading home.'

I start to walk off, but Ed calls me back. 'Don't just leave. We need to talk. Earlier, with my mum—'

'I know, I know . . .' I reply. 'But fuck, Ed! This whole thing is bullshit. Why did I suggest we come here and pretend everything is fine? It isn't fine, it's far from fine . . . and why the hell did you agree?'

'I don't know,' he admits. 'I didn't want to but—'

'Then tell me that! I may be insecure but you're so bloody spineless sometimes, it bores me to death. Tell me no! Be assertive! Choose the hard path sometimes. At least at work I have people who challenge me.'

'Challenge you?' he exclaims. 'They don't challenge you; they drive you insane! I can't remember the last time you didn't come home bitching and moaning.'

'Well, it's better than coming home with nothing to say at all,' I reply. 'At least I share my day. I literally have no idea what a day for you entails.'

'That's because you never ask!' he yells, throwing his hands in the air. 'And as for being spineless, I'm not the one too fucking gutless to tell the man you live with that you're not happy. To let him tiptoe around you for months, snapping at him. To allow him to think that it's just the job you don't love when in fact, it's him, too.'

'Ed, I never said—'

He shakes his head. 'I'm done, Kate. I have no idea what my life will be like without you, but fuck me, it has to be better than this. Let's get the next couple of days out the way and move on.'

We walk home in silence, me following a couple of steps behind to give him some space. He opens the door and heads straight to the living room while I go downstairs to bed. As I take off my jacket, I catch a glove that falls from my pocket, only it's not my glove. It's Ed's. I feel a sharp pang in my chest. Even after everything, he still doesn't want me to be cold. Goddammit. Why does he have to be so bloody decent?

2010

Kate

'It won't work.'

'Of course it will,' I tell Ed. 'People do it all the time.'

'OK, then. Tell me one long-distance relationship that has ever worked—'

'Jennifer Lopez and—'

'And not some bullshit celebrity couple who can nip over to see each other on gold-plated jets.'

'Dammit.'

Last week, everything was so simple. We both got our university acceptance letters on the same day and we even opened them together. We'd both applied to Durham University, among others – me for law and Ed for music – and we were both accepted. We had it all worked out; we'd find cheap student digs, get crappy part-time jobs and have the best three years of our lives.

But this morning, Ed got a second acceptance from Manchester Uni. His first choice. Things just became a lot less simple.

'Oh!' I exclaim. 'Ross Tucker and that girl he met on holiday. They went out all through sixth form.'

Ed chortles. 'Oh yeah, she was totally real, not made up at all.'

'What do you mean?'

'I mean, what twenty-five-year-old model wouldn't fall for a seventeen-year-old short arse on holiday in Tenerife with his parents?'

'But . . . but he had those photos. He had his arm around her!'

Ed grins. 'His cousin. Turns out his aunt is an ex-pat over there. I hear his mum went mental that he was telling everyone he shagged his cousin.'

My jaw hits the floor. 'Noooo! Oh my god, that's so creepy. Why didn't I hear about this?'

'No idea. I thought everyone knew,' he replies, getting up to change the CD. 'Though I must admit that I was kind of relieved to find out. The thought of Ross fuckin' Tucker losing his virginity before me, was soul-destroying. The guy listens to Maroon 5.'

'Says the guy who just put on Art Brut for the millionth time. You listen to the weirdest shit.'

He jumps back on the bed beside me. 'Well, it's better than that weird woman you always play. I'd like to launch her CD into space.'

I thump him on the thigh. 'Do not force me to choose between you and Regina Spektor; you will lose. My love for her will span centuries, much further than one hundred and thirty-one miles . . .'

He plumps up his pillow and turns towards me. 'What do you mean?'

'I looked it up,' I confess. 'Durham to Manchester is one hundred and thirty-one miles. Ed, you've always wanted to study there and—'

'And I'll hardly ever get to see you,' he replies, turning on to his back. 'Fuck. Why couldn't they just have said no?'

'Because you're brilliant,' I reply without hesitation. It's true. I've never met someone so musically talented in my whole life. I can barely hold a note.

He sighs as I stroke his hair. 'Listen, I won't be the reason you don't go. It's only three years. We will be fine. I promise. I'm not going anywhere.'

'But you could meet someone,' he says softly. 'Some good-looking intellectual prick who likes Phil Spektor—'

'Regina.'

'And who fancies you just as much as I do.'

I turn the same colour as my hair. 'Shut up. You'll be in Manchester. There's like fourteen billion girls there who'd die to meet a hot, piano-playing musician.'

'I like how you omitted the clarinet.'

'But the point is, I trust you and you should trust me. OK?'

He kisses me and smiles. 'OK. I love you, you know that, right?'

I nod. 'It's understandable, I'm very loveable.'

'You two need anything?' I hear Yvonne shout from the top of the stairs. 'Me and Dad are just off to the garden centre.'

'We're good, Mum,' Ed yells back. 'Kate brought enough heroin to last us at least three hours.'

'Edward Morrison, don't make me come down there.'

It always amuses me the way that Ed's mum and dad still treat him like he's a kid. It took them three years to allow us to be in the basement with the door closed.

'It's going to be weird,' I say, looking around. 'We've been hanging out in your bedroom since we were fourteen.'

'I know,' he replies. 'Best four years ever. Pretty sure my mum will just take a flamethrower to it when I leave.'

'Or she'll turn it into an Eddie shrine,' I mock. 'Wall-to-wall baby photos, crusty sheets left on the bed . . . discarded socks sticking to—'

'Oh god, enough!' he exclaims. 'You're so gross.'

'Me? They're not *my* socks.'

He hits me with a pillow and laughs, though his cheeks are more than a little red.

'Seriously, though . . . she'll really miss you. They both will. You're their little miracle.'

'I know,' he agrees. 'But Manchester isn't that far . . .'

I throw my arms around him and squeeze. 'It's the right thing to do.'

He nods. 'I know. Fuck, it'll just be weird not seeing you every day.'

'You'll cope. I'll send photos if I can get them back from Ross Tucker . . .'

He laughs. 'God, wait till I tell Carly. She's already had her acceptance. At least I'll know one person there.'

My squeeze loosens a little. 'Carly?'

'Yeah. The girl I met at music camp two years ago, remember? We email every now and again.'

'Oh,' I reply, casually. 'I don't remember you mentioning her. That's cool, though.'

As we continue to hug, I feel my stomach twist. Who the hell is Carly? Is she why Manchester is his first choice?

I hear him breathe a sigh of relief while I take a deep breath in. Maybe persuading him to go to Manchester isn't such a great idea, after all. Shit.

DECEMBER 25TH – CHRISTMAS DAY

Ed

I can't remember the last Christmas morning when I didn't awaken to the sound of Mum singing holier-than-thou carols in the wrong key. Today's choice of ear assassination is 'Once in Royal David's City'. I hear Dad hum the occasional *bum bum bum* as he potters about in the kitchen.

Kate's already up and in the shower, her Christmas clothes laid out on the chair at the window. The purple top she bought last week and black trousers. She suits purple. As with Mum's singing, I can't remember the last Christmas morning when Kate didn't kiss me the moment she woke up. Although I'm glad I said what I did last night, there's a little voice in my head reminding me that I've hurt the woman I love.

I'm getting dressed into my blue shirt and jeans as Kate appears from the shower, a towel wrapped loosely around her while she uses another to dry her hair. As she turns and her towel slips a little, my arousal is immediate and unexpected. Turns out my penis is nowhere near as upset with her as the rest of me.

I carefully button up my jeans and move to the living room, where Mum and Dad are busy sorting through presents. I see a stack for us and other gifts for their friends around the village.

'Merry Christmas!' I say in my best, my-life-is-not-an-utter-shambles voice. 'I see Santa's been.'

'Merry Christmas, Edward!' they say in unison. 'Where's Kate? We're just getting the gifts ready.'

'Shower,' I tell Mum. 'She won't be long.'

'Is she OK?' Mum says, almost in a whisper. 'I mean, it's none of my business but—'

'She's fine. Just a lot on her mind. You look lovely, Mum.'

'Well, isn't that nice, thank you, darling,' she says, twirling around to show off her dress. 'It's only Marks and Sparks but it hides all me lumps and bumps. Tuck your shirt in, love – it looks so much smarter. Oh, must check on the pastries.'

I refuse to explain to my mother on Christmas Day that my shirt is actually covering my erection and therefore won't be getting tucked in anytime soon, so I just mumble about feeling more comfortable this way and hope that's enough. Dad, unsurprisingly, is wearing yet another Christmas jumper, but he has a shirt and tie underneath. Smart yet fun. That's my dad to a tee.

'Nice snowman, Dad,' I state, sitting beside him on the couch. 'Think that's my favourite so far. Any tea on the go?'

'Thanks, son,' he replies, with a chuckle. 'I think I drank the last, but I'll refill. Oh, there she is! Merry Christmas, Kate. We're just going to make some tea.'

'Merry Christmas,' she replies, carrying a pile of presents. 'I completely forgot to bring these up yesterday. Shall I just put them under the tree?'

'Could *you* not have brought those up?' Mum asks, frowning at me. 'Big, strong lad like you could have carried them in one hand.'

'Oh, it's no problem,' Kate remarks. 'They're not heavy.'

She sounds remarkably chipper. I watch her place our presents under the tree, thinking how pretty she looks in that top with her natural curls hanging loose, instead of straight and sleek. I love her hair like this. It reminds me of the Kate I used to know, the Kate who would make me laugh until my face hurt and look at me with such passion that it made me weak. While she might have grown tired of looking at me, the feeling isn't mutual.

'I'll just help Mum,' Dad says, obviously trying to give us some space. 'Won't be long.'

Kate sits on the chair near the television. 'Merry Christmas, Ed.'

'Merry Christmas,' I reply, coolly. 'What time do we need to leave for your mum's?'

'I said we'd be there for eleven.'

I bob my head in acknowledgement. She might seem more cheerful this morning, but I can tell she hasn't slept well. Her eyes look a little puffy.

'Right, you two, tea, coffee and cinnamon swirls,' Mum announces, placing a tray on the sideboard. 'I know you're eating at Paula's later, so I've kept it light.'

Oh god. I forgot we're eating at Kate's mum's. As much as I like Paula, her cooking generally ranges from tolerable to inedible. Every year she makes me something vegetarian from scratch. Last year she served up cauliflower and Cheddar pie with roast potatoes and veg which was nice – until I found out later that she'd roasted the potatoes in lard.

'I just want to apologise for last night,' Kate says, meekly. 'I've been stressed lately, which is no excuse for my rudeness but—'

'Apology accepted,' Mum says, giving Kate a hug. 'We all get a bit narky at times, sweetheart, don't worry. You just take care of yourself, yeah? Now, these presents aren't going to unwrap themselves, are they?'

The gift exchange is easy enough. Dad loves his new fishing pole; Mum is elated with her bee hotel for the garden, and as usual, I get cash, as apparently, I'm both poor and impossible to buy for. Kate receives a Molton Brown gift set and a spa voucher which she seems delighted with. Dad's gift for Mum is the most surprising. He's had two diamonds and a ruby added to her wedding band, for the forty years they've been together.

'Dinner at the Savoy, then drinks in a pub . . . gosh, I forget the name . . . and home by midnight,' Dad informs Kate, while Mum sits blubbering beside him. 'I couldn't believe my luck that this gorgeous blonde agreed to go out with an ugly git like me. I knew that night that I'd marry her if she'd have me.'

I've heard this account of their first date a million times and it still makes me smile. Kate's smiling, too. At last, a tale of love and marriage that doesn't make her want to murder everyone. However, today I'm realising that my mum and dad's story is undoubtedly quite unique, and despite my best efforts, probably not one that I'm going to be able to emulate. The thing is, I don't see how I'll ever love anyone else as much as I love Kate.

Kate

As we say goodbye, I'm a little tearful. Not just because of what's been happening with Ed but because I snapped at Yvonne. That woman has been nothing but sweet and welcoming to me for the past fifteen years and I behaved like a brat.

'We'll be down again soon,' Ed says, hugging his parents. 'Enjoy the rest of your Christmas.'

'We will,' Dad responds. 'We're going to Patrick and Helen's for lunch this year. Save your mum's hands from getting too tired.'

'Chris!' Yvonne snaps. 'Don't be bothering Eddie with that. My hands are fine, sweetheart.'

Yvonne's had rheumatoid arthritis in her hands since her late fifties, to the point where she had to stop playing piano. That was hard for her. It was hard for Ed, too – the sight of his mum sitting at the piano by the living-room window wasn't one he was ready to let go of.

'I thought those meds were working?' Ed asks, glancing

at his dad, who lowers his head. 'And the physio? Mum, tell me.'

She sighs. 'The meds do help, sweetheart, and the steroids . . . but I'm getting on a bit. My fingers get stiff, joints swell up. It's nothing new and it's nothing to worry about; your dad's just fussing.'

'Let him fuss,' he says, kissing her on the cheek. 'Promise? And if you need anything, let me know, OK? I'll be checking up on you.'

Chris helps us with our bags while Ed starts to defrost the car. It's been cold enough for snow since we arrived, but still nothing except icy pavements and the very likely possibility that I'll fall on my arse at any moment. One more hug goodbye and we set off for Hope.

Hope and Castleton are very similar, only Hope has a far prettier name and doesn't have a massive great farting cave to attract tourists. It's centred right in the middle of Hope Valley and the Peakshole Water runs from here and into the affectionately named 'River Styx' at the Peak Cavern. Everything is very old and very slow here, even more so than in Castleton. They still get plenty of tourists who enjoy walking up hills and then back down again, but Castleton definitely has a more lively buzz. They do, however, have a four-star hotel and spa near by, which is always full when I visit and I'm starting to resent them for it.

The short journey to Mum and Gary's is as frosty as the

road we drive on. Part of me feels sorry for Ed, knowing that he's now going to be in my position, keeping up appearances for someone else's family. He does have a better temperament than me, however. I'm sure he'll hold it together.

We've barely made it into the hallway before Tom appears, sprinting towards us wearing a red jumper and a large green mask.

'Merry Christmas, Tom!'

'HULK SMASH!' he shrieks, bypassing me completely to rugby tackle Ed.

'Merry Christmas, little man,' Ed replies laughing, his voice muffled by the eight-year-old climbing on his face. 'I surrender, I surrender!'

'Let them get in the door,' I hear Gary yell from the living room. I step over Ed and Tom, rescuing the bag of presents before it gets squashed entirely.

'Merry Christmas!' I say, plonking the bag down beside the couch. 'If I'd known the Hulk was here, I'd have put on some body armour.'

'Merry Christmas, Kate,' Mum says, pulling me in for a hug.

'Don't you look sparkly!' I say, being careful not to dislodge any of the five thousand sequins on her jumper. 'I feel underdressed now.'

'Nonsense,' she replies. 'Did you forget your straighteners? You can borrow mine if you like.'

'No,' I reply, disregarding her obvious dig at my hair. 'Just couldn't be bothered taming the beast this morning.'

'Merry Christmas, Kate. I won't hug you yet, I'm covered in god knows what.'

'Oh, you're cooking?' I say, admiring Gary's food-splattered apron. 'There's a first.'

Mum never lets anyone else cook at Christmas. Once a year she adopts this weird nineteen-fifties' housewife persona, taking over the kitchen that she barely uses the other three hundred and sixty-four days of the year.

'I just had my nails done,' Mum informs me, wiggling her fingers. 'I'm not stuffing anything with these bad boys.'

'Did anyone lose a superhero?'

I turn to see Ed carrying a giggling Tom upside down into the living room. They both look adorable. Even upside down, I can see Tom eyeing the gifts in our bag. He gets his presents before Christmas lunch as it's unfair to make him wait all day to open them with the adults in the evening.

'That depends,' I reply. 'Do superheroes like presents because I think I have some around here . . .'

Mum leaves to pick up my grandma at two. My grandma (or Gubba, the name I gave her when I was one and couldn't say grandma) recently moved into sheltered housing in Bamford and her eighty-one-year-old face has been tripping her ever since. I don't blame her. She sold her beautiful cottage in Castleton and was forced to reside alongside 'those bloody coffin dodgers' as she lovingly calls the other residents. Ed and I visited the complex when she moved in, and it's surprisingly nice. Around twenty flats all built around a communal garden, with a community hall, lounge and a bus stop right outside. The flats are all brand new and everything is accessible, but it just reminds Gubba that she's older now and needs extra help, as much as it pains her to admit it. Mentally, she's as sharp as ever, but her legs don't hold her up quite as well as they used to, especially since falling last year and breaking her ankle in two places.

The sleeping arrangements have changed since last year, with Mum and Gary now in the new loft conversion and Tom in their old bedroom, which leaves Ed to lug our bags upstairs to the bedroom that used to be Tom's but also mine. They haven't redecorated yet, meaning that Ed and I will be forced to sleep surrounded by Marvel wallpaper and a dinosaur lamp. Gubba always sleeps on the sofa bed, claiming it's better for her back than Mum's *billowy mattress*, but also, it's nearer to the bathroom.

I wander into the kitchen and slice into the baguette that's sitting on the worktop beside the biggest jar of Nutella I've ever seen. This is the only advantage I can see to having kids, I think, scooping some on to my bread. Well, that and seeing their faces when they're opening Christmas presents. That melts my heart. I've never seen anyone so thrilled to get a Fortnite gift card and a Thor hoodie. Munching on my bread and chocolate I watch

Gary and Tom from the kitchen window, now joined by Ed. Seems he'd rather stand in the cold than be alone with me. Gary crouches down, followed by everyone else, as he points towards the grass about five feet to the left of him. I stand on my tiptoes and catch sight of a robin, pecking at the ground near by before being startled by Ed sneezing, losing his balance and Tom laughing his head off. Gary walks over to his magnificent copper bird table and starts filling up the little feeding stations, while Ed and Tom kick a ball around the garden. For a moment, I'm taken back to watching Ed on the football field at school. I never had any interest in football, I just liked the way he looked in shorts. He was so exciting to me back then, and to a lot of the other girls, which bothered me. He was fit, musically gifted, handsome as hell – but most of all, he was a great guy. No bravado, no ego, just funny and kind, and I couldn't figure out for the life of me, why he was into me. Maybe there's part of me, deep down, that still can't. Watching him, I realise that he isn't outside in the cold to avoid me. He's outside to be with Tom. He's out there playing with my eight-year-old brother at Christmas while I'm alone in the kitchen making everything all about me. Shit. I don't like this version of me at all.

Ed

I'm about to let Tom win his sixth game when I hear Paula yell that Gubba is here. Tom abandons the ball and zips back inside, knowing that more Christmas presents are on the cards, leaving me to score my first goal of the day.

'I'll be there in a minute,' Gary says, fiddling with the bird table. 'I'm just replacing the battery in this solar light.'

'No probs,' I reply, smiling. Gary is the first and only bird watcher (or 'twitcher', as he likes to call himself) I've ever known, and probably the most mellow bloke on earth. He's at least a decade older than Paula, which was a source of great embarrassment to Kate when her mum first introduced him. My folks are both older, so to me it was no big deal but compared to her dad, she thought Gary was practically ancient.

He owns a garden centre, Ed! My mum still goes clubbing, for god's sake. He must be loaded or something. It'll never last. She'll eat him alive.

But it did last, as did his garden centre, which everyone around here, including my parents, speak very highly of. Kate was right, of course; he was loaded, and she wasn't the only one in the village who thought Paula was taking advantage of the poor widowed twitcher, but my mum always said something that stuck with me.

Sometimes, the only way to leave chaos behind is to grab hold of calm and never look back.

Having met Brian, Kate's dad, this made perfect sense. Paula didn't fall in love with Gary for his money. She's never once asked him to move somewhere bigger, or upgrade her car; Christ, she still works part-time at the post office. She fell in love with him for his heart.

I can already hear Tom whooping as he rushes inside, followed by Gubba laughing. I feel so stupid calling her Gubba, instead of Grandma, or even her actual name, Marian, but everyone else does, so I just play along.

'Merry Christmas!' I say, giving her a hug before taking a spot on the couch beside Kate. 'Lovely to see you, Gubba. You look well.'

'Do I heck,' she replies, handing Tom another gift. 'I'm holding on to water like a bloody camel. Could hardly get me shoes on.'

'Camels don't wear shoes,' Tom informs her, unwrapping his gift.

Gubba laughs and nods. 'Aye, true,' she replies. 'Now if they're the wrong size, your mother will change them.'

Tom holds up a pair of Adidas Hulk trainers and begins whooping again.

'Queen's on in five minutes, Mum. You want a sherry?'

'Small one, ducky,' she tells Paula. 'Don't want to be bladdered in front of Lizzy.'

Everyone laughs. Gubba's a huge fan of the Royal Family (well, except Andrew) and insists that we all watch Her Majesty address the nation before lunch. My mum's the same. For them it's the highlight of Christmas, just as Charlie Brooker's New Year round-up is for Kate and me . . . damn, the thought of never doing that again makes me feel sick to my stomach. Just us on the couch, a bottle of wine, those godawful Twiglets she loves, and the sound of her laughter drowning out mine.

Kate

Just as the broadcast ends, Gary heads back to the kitchen. 'Lunch will be about another half hour,' he informs us. 'Sorry, running a bit behind. Those potatoes just aren't crisping up.'

'Need any help?' I ask. 'I can set the table in the dining room.'

'No, love, it's all done,' Gary informs me.

Ed gives a little snigger. God, he's so obnoxious sometimes.

'Something funny?' I ask him.

'Not really,' he replies. 'I just think it's the first time I've heard you offer to help in the kitchen. It's a Christmas miracle! God bless us, everyone!'

Now Mum's laughing. I tut and turn back to the telly.

'Have a walk with me,' Gubba suggests, giving me a nudge. 'These old legs need stretching.'

'But it's freezing,' Mum exclaims. 'You'll catch your death.'

'Death'll catch me either way,' Gubba replies, getting up. 'Stop fussing. We won't be long. I've got me stick and me snow boots.'

I grab my coat and help Gubba with hers, taking her arm as we step out into the garden, thankful to be away from Captain Snarky. Gary has placed little solar lights down the garden path which leads to a gate at the bottom and on to a country lane. It's not quite dark yet but it's getting there.

'Just up to the top and back,' she directs. 'That should be enough time.'

'Enough time for what?'

'For you to give me one of your cigs and tell me what's going on with you and Ed.'

Nothing gets past this woman.

'You're not supposed to be smoking,' I say, taking two cigarettes from my pack.

'No one is supposed to be smoking,' Gubba replies. 'It's bad for you. Oh, don't tell your mother – you know she gets her anti-smoking knickers in a knot, and we'll end up having a barney.'

I light her cigarette before my own. 'I won't say a word,' I promise. 'I stopped for ages but then ... ugh, Gubba, everything's just been a real shitshow lately. Work ... me and Ed ...'

Gubba nods, taking a long drag as we walk along the lane. It's so quiet and peaceful here. I think I've forgotten what peaceful feels like.

'I can tell,' she replies. 'You've barely said two words to each other, except to snipe.'

'We had a huge fight in the car on the way here,' I confess. 'It's just not working anymore.'

'Why?'

'God, where do I start?' I reply, my eyes brimming. 'We just want different things. He wants marriage and kids and—'

'You don't?' Her hand reaches into my pocket for another cigarette.

'We're only twenty-nine, Gubba! I've got so much more that I want to achieve before I have to give everything up.'

Gubba frowns, lighting her second cig. 'You really think having a family means you have to give everything up?'

'Well, doesn't it? Mum gave up everything for me.'

We've already walked to the end of the lane. She pauses for a moment before turning around to head back home.

'Kate, if you think you'll end up like your mother, you're mistaken – because your mother has worked hard and sacrificed to ensure that won't happen.'

'No, I didn't mean—'

'You did,' she interrupts, stubbing out her cigarette. 'And that's OK. No woman wants to end up like their mother, but every mother wants their child to do better than they did . . . that's the one part I thought I'd failed at. But when I see you and little Tom, I know that I haven't failed at all. Do you need a hanky?'

I nod, feeling warm tears streaming down my cold face. Like all good Gubbas, she produces a handkerchief from her coat pocket.

'I just thought there would be more to life than working in a job I hate and living with a man who seems to have settled for less than he's capable of.'

'There is,' she replies. 'Find a new job. If you're lucky, then life is bloody long, Kate. Don't waste it being miserable.'

'And Ed? What should I do?'

'Well, only you can decide that. But don't punish or nag him for not pushing himself.'

I wipe my nose and stuff the hanky back in my pocket, just as we reach the garden gate.

'He wasn't wrong about the kitchen remark, though,' she says. 'Even lawyers need to know how to peel a spud.'

And with that she marches on up the path. Damn, Gubba doesn't pull any punches.

We arrive back, just in time for me to help Gary bring the dishes through from the kitchen, while Gubba is shown to her seat by Mum.

The table looks incredible. As usual, Mum's outdone herself with a bright red cloth and a green runner along the length of the table, displaying oversized pine cones, holly shrubs and chunky red candles.

'I can carry a bloody gravy boat or something, Paula,' Gubba mumbles. 'Let me help. I'm not an invalid.'

'I know,' Mum replies. 'I just don't . . . what's that smell?' She sniffs Gubba's hair like a police-detection dog. 'Have you been smoking?'

Gubba and I exchange glances. She sighs, knowing that Mum's about to give her an earful.

'Just the one,' she replies. 'One of those great big wacky-baccy cigarettes, like we had in the sixties, wooo!'

Mum frowns as Gubba makes peace signs. 'This is not a joke. The doctor insisted you stop. You promised me! I cannot believe—'

'It was me,' I interrupt, putting the carrots on the table. 'I was smoking, Gubba just caught the backdraft. Sorry.'

I see the corners of Gubba's mouth turn upwards, though she tries not to make it obvious.

'Well, that's disappointing,' Mum says, stepping away from my chain-smoking grandmother. 'I'm really not sure that's any example to set your brother, and your grandma has bad lungs. What were you thinking?'

'I was thinking that I'm twenty-nine and I wanted a fag,' I reply. 'But you're right, I should have been more considerate. Tom – never smoke. It'll stunt your growth. I should be six foot instead of five foot five. And sorry, Gubba, for dragging you into all this.'

Gubba nods. 'Your mother's right, Kate. It's really very disappointing.'

Wow. My grandmother is kind of a dick. I try not to laugh, disappearing back into the kitchen to retrieve some more veg. Ed follows behind me, grabbing some serving utensils for the table.

'She was smoking too, right?' he whispers, leaning in as he reaches across for the tongs.

'Yup,' I reply. 'But no point in both of us enduring the wrath of my mother, eh?'

'You look great,' he says, still in a whisper and it sends a shiver up my spine. He's the only man I know who can make a simple compliment sound completely dirty. I may not be sure about my future with Ed, but it appears that my libido is quite certain where its loyalties lie. Get a fucking grip, Kate, I clear my throat before thanking him.

He smiles and starts to walk away but pauses at the door. 'Kate, I think we need to—'

'Will you two hurry up – we're starving in here!'

I grimace at the decibel level of my mum's voice. 'Just coming!' I shout back in a far more civilised tone.

'We can talk about whatever it is later,' I inform Ed. 'Jesus, her voice booms like she's about to climb down a frickin' beanstalk.'

Ed

I take my seat beside Kate as Gary brings in the turkey, smiling politely while everyone oohs and ahhs at the sight of a slaughtered animal. They're lucky I'm not at all militant about my vegetarianism, unlike my colleague Jane, the Religious and Moral Education teacher who likes to ambush carnivores in the staffroom and ask if they know how their lunch was killed.

Still, I'm looking forward to Christmas lunch, now that Gary has taken the reins. He's a tremendous cook anyway, and he even has his own vegetable patch and greenhouse. I once told Kate I'd like to get an allotment. She threatened to have me sectioned.

An allotment? Good grief, Ed, you're twenty-six. Do you also want to start pulling your trousers up to your nipples and go on a cruise?

My main course this year is a beetroot, Stilton and kale Wellington, which smells fantastic. Even Gubba considers trying some. While we all make conversation, I notice the familiar scent of the perfume Kate's used to mask the cigarette stench. It's the one I bought her for her birthday last year. The one she keeps for special occasions. The one she dabs on her finger, then runs between her—

'Breast or thigh?'

Fucking hell. Never has a question been timed so perfectly. I inadvertently laugh, causing everyone to look at me like I'm an idiot.

'Thigh,' Gary replies, while I snort into my napkin. 'You all right there, Ed?'

I nod, trying to compose myself. 'Sorry, just thought of something funny, ignore me.'

'Share it, then,' Gubba insists. 'I'm sure we'd all like a laugh.'

'Is it a joke?' Tom asks, stabbing a carrot. 'I know some jokes.'

Oh god. They're all staring. My urge to shout 'GUBBA SMOKED TOO' is overwhelming. Think, Ed, think! 'No, I was just thinking about that time when . . . Gubba set the Christmas pudding on fire.'

'Oh my god!' Paula exclaims. 'I'd forgotten about that!'

Tom stops eating and gasps. 'Gubba set the pudding on fire?'

Gary nods, offering his son some potatoes. 'Before you were born. It was the Christmas before Kate and Ed left for university. She set the fire alarm off and everything.'

'I did not,' Gubba insists, smirking. 'It was a gentle flame.'

'Oh, you did,' Kate interjects, laughing. 'You almost incinerated it. Gary was as white as a sheet, thinking we'd have to evacuate and call the fire brigade.'

Paula's almost in tears. 'Then he panicked and threw the trifle on it. The trifle!'

Even Gubba's in stitches. 'Aye, I might have been a smidge over eager with the brandy.'

'Do you have any funny stories about one of my Christmases?' Tom asks. He looks so innocent, even down to his blond hair. Well, maybe not so much today, as it's all messy and spiky, like a villain from the *Beano*.

I pause. I can't think of a single thing.

'When you were about four, you, me and Ed made the most amazing pillow fort.'

I finally turn to look at Kate.

'We did?' he asks. 'Where?'

'In your room,' she continues. 'We had pillows and cushions and blankets; it was brilliant! And it stayed up for three whole days. You even slept there when Santa came.'

'I think I remember that!' Tom exclaims. 'We had my football lamp inside and we watched *Duck Tales*.'

I catch Kate's eye. The *Duck Tales* theme tune is genuinely one of her favourite songs. She plays it in the car. When she's not being so damned stressed and miserable, she's the most adorable woman I've ever met.

Paula nods. 'You're right. I'd forgotten about that, too. I must have pictures somewhere; I'll take a look.'

'Why did we take it down?' Tom asks, obviously now intending to make another as soon as possible.

'Well, we needed the cushions and pillows back and—'

'Oh no,' I say to Paula. 'That's not the real reason.'

'It isn't?' she asks, side-eyeing everyone else.

'I think it's time Tom knows the truth about what *really* happened to his pillow fort,' I respond, cutting into my Wellington. 'You see, Tom, your big sister had a terrible cold that year. She was really sick – coughing and shivering and sneezing.'

Tom leans forwards, utterly captivated.

'And the only place she felt better was in your pillow fort. So we all slept there. But on the last night, her sneezing was out of control. She sneezed so forcefully that she accidentally farted at the same time and blew the entire fort down.'

'Ed!'

'He needs to know the truth, Kate. That his sister's fart practically blew us all into oblivion.'

Tom almost falls off his chair laughing, Gary is shaking so much, he's turning red and Paula and Gubba howl like a couple of banshees, while a horrified Kate thumps me on the thigh under the table.

'That's the funniest thing I've ever heard!' Tom exclaims and I agree, casually going back to my dinner.

'Only you could turn something so pure into a fart story,' Kate says, giving in to her laughter. 'Forever the teenage boy. Now, if you'll excuse me, I need to use the loo.'

She covers her ears as Tom starts blowing raspberries as she walks.

Kate

I've replied to five out of seven texts from Tara Mitchell
since this morning. I'm not sure why she thinks I work on
Christmas Day (other than the fact that I'm stupid enough
to reply to her texts on Christmas Day). Most annoyingly,
not one has been anything short of ridiculous and puerile.
From items she swears he's taken from the house without
permission (including a jade face roller and a Yoni egg) to
him being ten minutes late bringing back the kids, even
though Newcastle is currently under four foot of snow. I
know this is the job I signed up for, but I didn't sign up
to be a doormat, and between my bosses and my clients,
that's exactly how I feel.

> Just email me the details and we can discuss when I'm back in the
> office. Anything else, please ram it up your arse.

I delete the last part and press send before hiding my
phone back behind the toilet brush. I flush the loo and

wash my hands to make my trip here sound authentic, though I'm sure Tom's expecting the roof to blow off after Ed's idiotic story. As much as I hate being the butt of a joke (no pun intended), I must give Ed credit. From pillow forts to flatulence jokes, he knows how to make memories for my little brother.

Thankfully, when I get back to the dining room, the conversation has moved on to something else.

'No way,' Tom sneers. 'I hate girls.'

'What are we talking about?' I ask, stabbing my fork into a sprout.

'Well, Tom got a gift from a girl in his class and Ed was just asking if she was his girlfriend,' Gary replies. 'It would appear the answer is a firm no.'

'Who gave you a gift?'

'Paige Rayner,' he mumbles. 'She gave me some Pokémon cards.'

'Well, I think that was very nice of her,' Gubba interjects. 'Thoughtful.'

Tom shrugs. 'I already had those ones.'

'Not often you see girls giving presents to boys,' Gubba continues. 'Not in my day, anyway.'

'I remember the first Christmas present you gave to me,' Ed says, while I'm in the middle of chewing. 'Do you?'

It takes me a second, but I get there. 'Oh god, don't tell that story.'

'You just spat sprout at me,' he says, brushing down his shirt.

'That's how much I don't want you to tell that story.'

'Shh,' Gubba tells me. 'I want to hear it.'

Ed grins, while I cringe so hard my face hurts. 'So Kate and I hadn't been officially dating for very long. I mean, we were friends, but it took me over a year to pluck up the courage to ask her out. Anyway, we were fifteen and had no money, so for our first Christmas, Kate made me a mixtape, well, mix-CD, of all my musical heroes.'

Mum awws, while Tom wonders what a mixtape is. When he's fifteen, they'll probably be firing off holographic Spotify playlists directly into their crush's eyeballs. It wouldn't quite have the same significance, though.

'It was really something,' he continues. 'She'd put so much effort into it, even designing a little cover for it. I played the hell out of that thing. Best present ever.'

He turns and smiles, and I can't help but smile back. He's right. I worked my arse off making that. Back then I was completely nuts about Ed and I wanted to impress him. If I'd had the money, I'd have gold-plated that bad boy.

'But aren't mixtapes supposed to be a way of sharing your musical tastes with someone else?' Gary asks.

'Yeah,' I reply. 'But he would have hated my music and gone off me. My hope back then was that when he played his favourite songs, he'd think of me.'

'Well, it worked,' he admits. 'I still can't listen to "The Thong Song" without thinking of you.'

I laugh loudly. 'I did not put that song on there!'

Ed nudges me playfully. 'I know, I'm kidding. Besides, you know which song I'm thinking about and sorry, everyone, I have no intention of sharing what that is. That's ours.'

It's 'Something' by The Beatles. We've danced to that so many times. I briefly place my hand on his before glancing at Gubba. She raises her eyebrows and smiles. I know what she's thinking. Because I'm thinking it, too. Despite everything, there's still love there.

Finally finished with dinner, Gary asks if we're ready for dessert.

'Give it ten minutes, ducky,' Gubba tells him. 'I need to make some room. I'm bursting at the seams.'

'Kate and I will start clearing the table,' Ed suggests, already scooping up plates with one hand. 'Take a break, Gary.'

Three trips later, I begin loading the dishwasher, while Ed fills the sink with hot water to steep the dishes that are too big to fit.

'That was fun,' I say, trying to prise out a fork which has wedged in the cutlery basket.

'Yeah,' he agrees. 'Really enjoyed that.'

'Still can't believe you told them about my mixtape. That seems like a million years ago now. God, we were so young.'

'I still have it, you know,' Ed confesses. 'The CD.' He turns off the tap and laughs quietly. God, I was almost giddy when you gave me that.'

'And yet you never returned the favour,' I reply, finally dislodging the fork. 'Though we rarely played any of my songs, so you wouldn't have had a clue what to include.'

As I stand and close the dishwasher door, I feel Ed standing behind me. He places his hands on my shoulders.

'I know things are shit,' he begins. 'And I know this probably isn't a wise move.'

'What isn't?' I ask, before feeling him press up against me. 'Oh.'

He moves my hair off my shoulder and leans in. I feel his breath on my neck. He doesn't say anything, he just sighs, but that sigh makes every part of my body tingle. I lean back into him and tilt my head, desperate for him to move his mouth to my neck. Which he does. Soon his hands are exploring my body and I have no intention of stopping them.

'Ahem, shit, sorry. Just wanted to check the oven.'

Ed and I both snap back to reality, blushing like a couple of teenagers, while I readjust my top. 'No probs,' I laugh. 'Just too much vino. I'll leave you to it.'

I rush out of the kitchen and back to the dining room. My heart is beating so fast, I fear I might pass out. God, I think I still fancy my boyfriend.

Ed

I sheepishly nod to Gary as I leave, pulling down my shirt to cover any lingering evidence of how turned on I was two minutes ago. As much as I want to disembowel Gary with a rusty spoon for interrupting us, I cannot imagine how he felt, seeing his stepdaughter getting groped in his own kitchen.

I nip to the toilet to clear my head which is spinning. For a moment there, we felt like us. Like the people we used to be, uncomplicated and unable to keep our hands off each other. It feels like we're both trying here. It feels like maybe—

I'm interrupted by a faint buzzing sound. No, not a buzz – more of a vibration. I follow the sound behind me, reaching behind the toilet brush. Kate's phone with three new WhatsApp messages from Tara. Her client. She's been sneaking work calls the whole holiday. I put the phone back and leave the bathroom.

Everyone has decided to have dessert while we open our

presents. I briefly lock eyes with Kate as I enter the room but do my best to avoid Gary's until he makes contact first. Tom is sitting beside Kate, so I park myself next to Gubba, who playfully slaps my knee.

'My Tom was about your height,' she tells me. 'Big six-footer. We looked ridiculous together, what with me only being five foot two in me heels.'

Gubba's told me this numerous times but it's not because she's getting on a bit; it's because she's slightly pissed. That sherry bottle will be in her handbag by the end of the evening.

'Right, everyone, I thought we'd have something a little different this year,' Gary announces. 'We have panettone with mascarpone and non-flammable figgy-pudding-flavoured ice cream.'

He lays the desserts out on the table and stands back to admire his work. I don't blame him; the whole concept is a thing of beauty.

The annual Christmas-gift exchange is pleasant enough, with everyone pretending to love their gifts a little more than they actually do. I'm off the hook, as Kate picked out the gifts for her family, so I cannot be held responsible. Gubba, of course, brings everyone back to reality by asking Paula what in the hell made her buy a 'Born in the 40s' sweetie box when she hasn't had her own teeth in years.

'How am I supposed to eat Bonfire Toffee with dentures

in, Paula? Give it to the wee fella. He still has his baby teeth.'

Finally, as I hand Kate her gift, I start to panic a little. The timing couldn't be more unfortunate, given our current situation.

Before I can make up an excuse, she starts to open it. My wrapping skills aren't the greatest but with Kate it doesn't matter anyway, as she claws at the paper without even looking.

'A scrapbook?' she asks, looking confused, probably because she's been hinting for months about a pair of Vivienne Westwood earrings she's absolutely in love with.

'Yep,' I reply. 'It's nothing, really.'

She tentatively opens the blue cover and pauses, staring at the first photo.

'Who's that?' Paula asks, peering across the room.

'It's us,' she replies, her voice breaking a little. 'Me and Ed. At school.'

She starts flipping through the pages, running her fingers across every memory of us I could find. The notes we passed in class, which I kept, the ticket stubs from the Reading Festival where she lost her favourite sunglasses headbanging to Metallica, photos from our school hoedown, the booking receipt from the dodgy hotel we stayed at when I visited her for a weekend in Durham, even the cinema ticket stubs from the first time we hung out together outside of school. It's a history of us.

'Do you like it?' I ask, noticing that she hasn't said a word. She starts to cry.

'Kate?'

'I'm sorry,' she says, closing the book. She grabs my gift and leaves the room, almost at a sprint. I can still hear her sobbing as she goes upstairs. I immediately follow her up.

I go into the bedroom and close the door behind me. Kate's sitting facing the window with her back to me, her head in her hands.

'Look, I know the book was bad timing,' I say. 'It wasn't even your proper gift, I'd just forgotten all about it, until—'

'I'm just so sad, Ed,' she responds. 'Looking through that book ... I just can't get my head around the fact that it's over.'

I sit on the opposite side of the bed with my back to her. 'You wanted this, Kate,' I remind her. 'I'm not the one who suggested we split.'

'I know,' she replies, sniffing loudly. 'I was just so frustrated ... not only with us, but with everything. I feel stuck, Ed. And confused. I have all these feelings and ... I mean ... in the kitchen ...'

Her voice trails away and she starts to cry again.

'I still want you, Kate,' I say. 'That hasn't changed.' I position my hand beside hers. 'But you were right. There is something broken between us. It was unfair of me to have a go at you for not saying anything sooner because I didn't say anything either.'

I feel her fingers intertwine with mine and I try to hold back my own tears.

'I found your phone in the bathroom,' I confess. 'I know you've still been working.'

She sighs. 'Ed, I don't want to go over this again.'

'I know. It just didn't make me feel good that you felt you had to hide it from me. I don't want to live like that.'

'Neither do I.'

We sit quietly, fingers interwoven, just listening to the sounds on the street outside and the low mumble from the television downstairs.

'Is there any way we can save this?' I ask.

'I don't know,' she replies softly. 'We still want such different things, Ed. I'm not sure that will ever change.'

I give her hand a gentle squeeze before turning to face her. God, her beautiful face.

'I love you, Kate.'

She wipes her eyes and smiles. 'I love you, too, Ed. Regardless of what happens, I really, really fucking love you.'

We kiss for the first time since we arrived in Castleton, but it's bittersweet and we both know it. She pulls away first, leaning her forehead against mine.

'What a fucking Christmas,' she says, with a small laugh which breaks the tension.

'Tell me about it,' I reply. 'I'm so sorry that silly book made you cry.'

'No, the book is amazing,' she counters. 'But I was also crying because I got you such a shitty gift.'

She hands me the parcel and covers her face.

I tear open the wrapping and read the box: Ray Gun Nose Trimmer.

I start to laugh. 'Oh my god. I literally spent hours on that scrapbook!'

'We said only small gifts this year,' she replies, playfully pushing me as my laughter gets louder.

'Small gifts?' I ask, trying to catch my breath. 'You literally cut out a picture of Vivienne Westwood earrings and left it on my side of the bed. And I get this!'

'A girl can dream,' she replies, grinning. 'Besides, you have this one hair that drives me crazy. Sometimes when you breathe, it looks like it's waving at me.'

Now she's laughing, too, and we can't stop.

Finally, we're able to compose ourselves and decide to head back downstairs. We enter the living room, still giggling.

'Apologies, everyone,' Kate says. 'I got a little emotional. I'm good now.'

'We're going to watch *Paddington 2*!' Tom announces. 'Come and sit with me, Ed.'

Kate and I lock eyes for a second as Tom pulls me towards the couch. I know that technically nothing was resolved but I feel like a weight has been lifted. I pick up my melted dessert and sit down beside Tom. An hour later, he's snuggled up to me, fast asleep.

2013

Kate

'You don't have to come in, you know. No one would blame you. It's hardly the most exciting way to spend a Saturday afternoon.'

Ed turns the engine off and opens his door. 'Grab that bag, will you? I'll get the balloon.'

We've just driven from Ed's mum's house to my mum's with a giant, helium-filled teddy balloon, bouncing in the seat behind us, and I'm starting to think it was a massive mistake.

'He's going to hate it,' I say. 'I mean, look at it. It's grinning. Who the hell wants this floating in the corner of their room at night like some Build-A-Bear sleep-paralysis demon?'

Ed chuckles. 'Build-A-Scare.'

'Exactly,' I reply. 'I say we go back to yours and just Skype them or something. Or at least get a better gift and send it by courier. Maybe by then they'll actually have named the rugrat and we can skywrite his name or something.'

'You need to relax,' Ed insists. 'It's just a baby, Kate. Whether it's a balloon or a Ferrari, he won't give a shit. He won't even be able to see properly yet.'

We've been back in Castleton for a couple of months now, living in Ed's basement because my mum decided to get knocked up again at thirty-eight and has turned my room into a nursery. Eventually, they'll convert the loft into a bedroom but for now I'm left with Ed's house or the couch.

'How do you know about a baby's eyesight?' I ask. 'Have you been on Mumsnet again?'

He laughs. 'No . . . but how do you not know this?'

I don't know anything about babies which is my entire problem right now. I'm twenty-one and I've never even held one.

As I open the front door, I'm hit by the smell of soup. Gary must have been cooking; either that or my new brother smells like coriander. Do babies smell like coriander? Before I can ask Ed if that's a thing, Gary's head appears around the living-room door.

'Right on time,' Gary says, grinning. 'Come and meet Tom.'

Tom. That was my grandad's name. He died before I was born but I've heard he was a lovely man.

We walk into the living room where Mum is lying on the couch. Her hair is part bun, part firework explosion, and she looks like she hasn't slept in . . . well, ever. Beside her there's a small white Moses basket, which appears to be gently swaying on its own.

'How are you feeling, Mum?'

'Like I've been hit by a truck,' she replies, sitting up. 'But I'm all right. Don't stand on ceremony, you two. Come and see the boy wonder.'

I creep over to the crib and peer in. There, dressed all in blue, is Tom. Teeny, wrinkly, squishy-faced Tom. I don't think I've ever seen anything as perfect in my life.

Ed peeks in and grins. 'He's so cute! Lots of hair, like his dad, eh?'

Mum smiles. No, she beams. Even through the exhaustion, she looks happy. In fact, I don't think I've seen her as happy in a long time. 'Yeah, I was surprised. When Kate came out, she was bald. In fact, she was pretty much bald until she was about eight months old.'

'Think I'd rather have stayed bald,' I mumble, still staring at Tom. His mouth is open, making little croaky sounds while he bats his fists around. Mum sits forwards and lifts him up.

'Here,' she says, offering me Tom. 'Have a hold.'

I step back. 'Hold? I can't. How do I—'

'Like this,' Mum replies. 'Just be careful with his head.'

'He's too little!' I exclaim. 'He's wriggling. I'll drop him. Oh god, what if I drop him?'

'You won't.' Mum laughs and tries to hand Tom over

again. 'Come on, Kate, it'll be good practice for when you have kids.'

'Uh-uh.'

'He's your brother,' she insists. 'Don't be so silly!'

Utterly terrified, I hold Tom and stand like a statue. Tom looks up at me and for a moment we stare at each other. Then he starts to cry. Not just cry – he wails like a damn banshee.

'Why is he crying?' I ask, my eyes now as big as saucers. 'What did I do?'

'Nothing,' Mum replies. 'He's a baby, Kate. That's what they do.'

'He looked at me and started crying!' I proclaim, shooting a look at Ed. 'I thought you said babies couldn't see yet.'

Both Gary and Mum start to laugh, which doesn't make me feel any better about the situation. 'Can someone take him please?'

'Can I have a hold, Paula?'

I look at Ed, who's already holding his arm in the appropriate position. Mum takes Tom from me, kisses his face, then hands him to Ed.

'Hello, little man,' he coos, booping his tiny nose. 'What's all the fuss, eh?'

I watch in amazement as Tom immediately stops crying.

'Wow,' Gary remarks. 'Looks like you've got the golden touch, lad.'

Ed smiles and starts walking Tom around the room.

'Want to try again, Kate?' he asks, while Tom the traitor continues to coo at him.

'I'm good, Mary Poppins,' I reply. 'I'm just going to use the loo.'

I leave the room and head upstairs, peeking into my old bedroom. The walls are now yellow, with animal stencils all around them. A cot stands where my bed used to be, and near the window is a large white chest of drawers with a blue mat on top. Although we only moved in here two years before I left for uni, there's nothing left of me here. It's been gutted to make memories for someone else.

I go into the bathroom and close the door, locking it behind me. I wonder if I can just hide in here? This is very surreal, and I'm actually surprised that my mum wants to go through all this again. The crying and the feeding and the nappies . . . not to mention she'll be well into her fifties by the time Tom goes to university.

I finish using the loo and grab some toilet paper, noticing a big white packet on the shelf beside me. Maternity pads. I pull one out and wince. They're huge. Jesus, how much do you bleed after birth? This could absorb a pint of beer. I mean, my periods are heavy, but I couldn't picture myself wearing . . .

I pause.

My period. I begin running numbers and dates in my head. Last period? The day I met Lauren for coffee; I had to borrow some change for the tampon machine. That was the Saturday before Ed came home from Manchester and I wasn't on then because we had sex twenty-five times. Which was seven weeks ago. Which means . . . I'm late.

I run the dates again, then again, but the answer is still the same. I feel myself break into a cold sweat. This can't be right. There's no way I could be pregnant. We were careful, we've always been careful.

Fuck, were we careful?

No. No way. Careful people who are about to start a graduate diploma do not get pregnant. People who want to buy a brand-new red Mini convertible with absolutely no room in the back for a baby seat do not get pregnant!

I hear Ed downstairs, still talking in that stupid baby voice to Tom. Normally, I'd find this cute but right now him being excited by offspring is the last thing I need to hear. Right now, I'd rather hear him announce that he has *no plans to ever become a father and could someone please remove the baby from his field of vision*. The moment I share any of this with him, everything will change, whether I'm actually pregnant or not. I'm not ready to tell him that kids with me might never be an option.

Putting on my best game face, I return to the living room and perch on the end of the couch. I'd be lying if I said it wasn't strange being back home. Being back with Ed. We've spent the past three years adapting to a new way of being together, with endless phone calls, snatching weekends here and there in between holiday visits.

When we left for university, although it was difficult at first, there was a certain allure to what we were doing. We'd been together almost every day since we were fourteen, so the longing we felt, although almost unbearable, made our time together even more precious. However, inevitably the novelty of the first year soon wore off and after that, not seeing Ed became the norm. Even during the summer break, we both still had to work to ensure we didn't get thrown out of our respective flats and replaced with one of the many students trying to find decent accommodation for the next term, which meant seeing each other less and less. I spent a good chunk of my time at university wondering if what Ed had said was right – that long-distance relationships don't work.

But we battled on and now we're home again, right back where we started, and while Ed is the same funny, loveable, slightly irritating person he always was, it feels like something has changed. No, not something. Me.

DECEMBER 26TH – BOXING DAY

Kate

Despite the gargantuan amounts of food I consumed yesterday, I'm starving this morning. Gary's back in the kitchen and has prepared us all some bacon, eggs and slightly burnt toast. I pull out the seat next to Gubba and pour myself some tea.

'That perfume is lovely, Kate. What is it?'

'It's called Miss Dior, Gubba,' I reply, taking my third slice of toast. 'Ed bought me it for my birthday.'

'Can I borrow some?' she asks, sipping her tea. 'I haven't brought any with me.'

'Of course,' I say, finding it a tad strange. Gubba doesn't tend to wear perfume often these days as it irritates her skin. 'I'll get it for you after breakfast, before we leave.'

'You headed to *his* house?' Mum asks, handing Tom some cereal. She rarely calls my dad, Brian, by his first name. In fact, she usually calls him that useless tosser, but never in front of Tom.

'Yep, same as always,' I respond. 'I don't think anyone else visits him.'

'He made his bed,' she says, dipping her bacon into a bright yellow yolk. 'No sympathy here.'

Although Mum never tried to stop me seeing my dad after he left, she's never been exactly thrilled that I continue to see him whenever I'm home. Trying to explain to Mum that her relationship with him and my relationship with him are two very separate things is pointless. Even now she's married to Gary, I don't think she'll ever forgive my dad for the way he ended things.

After breakfast, I run upstairs to grab my perfume and take it to Gubba, who's finishing her tea in the living room.

'Here you go,' I say, holding out the bottle. 'It can be quite strong so—'

She takes the perfume and slips it into her cardigan pocket. 'Just going to get the papers,' she shouts to Mum. 'I'll bring back some blue-top milk. That skimmed stuff is just white water.'

'Get your coat,' she whispers. 'You're coming, too.'

It's a lot milder this morning as we step outside and there's barely any frost on the ground, though I'm more concerned that Gubba's just dragged me out in public with no make-up on.

'I do like a wee ciggy after breakfast,' she says, linking my arm with hers. 'But now that *mein Führer* is on her high horse about smoking, I'll have to cover me tracks, won't I?'

'So that's what the perfume is for,' I reply, laughing. 'God, this reminds me of being a teenager, when we'd all drench ourselves in cheap body spray to avoid detection.'

Gubba chuckles. 'Everyone smoked in my day. It was just the done thing, though my mother hated it with a passion. She forbade me to even look at a cigarette. She'd smell my fingers when I came in of an evening.'

Gubba and I have a leisurely stroll to the newsagents and back. She's definitely not as light on her feet as she used to be, but she still powers on. I've never really thought of her as old, until recently. I remember when I was a kid, around five or six, we'd jump on the bus to Sheffield and spend the day exploring bookshops and museums, getting ice cream before heading home. I'd go to her house after school and at weekends when my parents were either off on a night out or at home fighting and she never once said a bad word about either of them – well, not in front of me at least. Best grandma ever.

As we near the house, Gubba sprays my perfume over both of us, like she's putting out a fire. 'Woah, easy there, Gubba. That's a hundred quid a bottle!'

'For this?' She examines the bottle, closely. 'That boy must love you, eh?'

I take the bottle and smile. 'Yeah, he does.'

'Then I certainly wouldn't be in any great hurry to let him go.' We get to the gate, and I smirk as she gives her fingers one last spritz. 'And I don't think you are . . . are you?'

I shake my head. 'I hope we can work it out Gubba. I really do.'

She gives me a hug and kisses my cheek. 'You will, ducky and you know where I am if you need to talk. Now off you go and visit your dad. I'm going to get Gary to run me home now. We're playing bingo in the community hall and there's a bottle of Croft up for grabs.'

An hour later, Ed and I are ready to go, as is Gubba who's already sitting in Gary's car with her coat buttoned up to the neck and her house keys in her hand. Tom isn't so keen on us leaving, but he never is.

'But we didn't get to play Fortnite,' Tom whines, as Ed hugs him goodbye. 'Can't you stay a bit longer?'

'Aww, mate, I'm sorry. Listen, how about next time I'm up, we spend the whole day together. We could go swimming or to the zoo?'

'Or play Fortnite?'

'Yes,' Ed laughs. 'Or play Fortnite.'

I used to be somewhat miffed that Tom was never really that sad to see me leave while he practically held on to Ed's leg in protest, but now I understand why. I might be his sister by blood, but Ed's the best big brother in the world. I could offer to take Tom to space on the back of a talking elephant and he'd probably pass unless Ed was coming, too.

'I'll miss you,' I tell Tom, hugging him. 'Please send me some of your drawings from school so I can put them on the fridge like last year.'

He agrees, sulking and mumbling something about a battle bus, until I see Ed whisper and make a 'shh' gesture with his finger. He nods and grins enthusiastically.

'See you at Easter,' I tell Mum and Gary, giving them a joint hug. 'Take care.'

'You too,' Mum replies. 'And you, Ed. Take care of each other.'

We pack the car, beep goodbye and embark on the final stop of our Christmas tour. The one I've been dreading the most. Brian Ward, my problematic father extraordinaire.

2010

Kate

'Mum would have a conniption if she saw this place,' I tell Ed as we pull up across the street from Dad's new flat. My heart hurts for her. She's always wanted to move to a new build but somehow Dad convinced her that they were boring and charmless; he preferred a character property, like our house in Castleton. It appears he's changed his mind. This place is barely out of the wrapper.

'Yeah, it's bigger than his last flat,' Ed replies, brushing some dust off the dashboard before wiping a non-existent smudge from the windscreen with the sleeve of his jumper. 'Though that wouldn't be hard. Place was like a shoebox . . . does this look smudged to you?'

For the past week Ed's been obsessed with his new car, a spotless Volkswagen Golf, which his mum and dad bought for him last month. I passed my test six months ago but the only way my mum could get me a new car is if she stole Ed's. Still, at least he'll be able to drive up and see me from Manchester.

'It's good, babe,' I tell him. 'You're literally wiping nothing.'

'Just keeping Kiki clean,' he replies, grinning. Honestly, sometimes I think boys live on another planet. Here I am, about to visit my dad and his new girlfriend in his new flat and he's more interested in wiping a lump of metal he's given a name to.

We exit the car and dash across the road to the flats on the other side. There are at least twenty sandstone brick flats here, and what looks like an automatic barrier for private parking to the right of us. The first flat he moved into after he left Mum, was a one-bedroom cottage flat that didn't even have central heating. Regardless, my dad always seems to land on his feet, I'll say that for him.

I look down the names on the entry buzzers.

6/1 B. Ward

This place better have a lift, I think to myself as I push the button. *I'm not walking up six flights of stairs in heels for anyone.*

'Hello?'

'Hi, Dad, it's us.'

'Who's us? Not sure I know any us.'

I sigh. He's either being intentionally annoying or he's been drinking. Probably both. 'Just buzz me in, will you,' I reply. 'I need the loo.'

The door clicks open, I'm hit by a strong paint smell as we walk into a small, bright, entrance hall with a lift directly in front of us and stairs to the right. Ed presses the button, and we wait. Part of me hopes the lift is broken so that I'll have my first negative thing to tell Mum when I get home.

'I'm really not looking forward to this,' I tell Ed as the lift starts to move.

'I know,' he replies. 'We don't have to stay long.'

The paint smell hits us again as the lift doors open on floor six. A long cream-coloured hallway greets us with three flats on the right. As I knock on the door to Dad's new flat, I'm reminded of our old front door at home with the crack across the bottom and the peeling green paint. Another thing Dad said he'd get around to fixing.

'Katie!' he exclaims, pulling open the door. 'And Eddie! Come in, come in.'

I can sense Ed tense up. He hates being called Eddie almost as much as I hate being called Katie. 'Hey, Dad,' I reply, as we step inside. 'Where's your loo?'

'End of the hall but I think—'

My attention is drawn to the sound of the toilet flushing.

'—Jane is in there.'

Mum and Dad have officially been over for two years, but I still think it's a bit soon for him to have shacked up with someone else.

'Come through to the lounge,' Dad insists. 'I've got us some beers in.'

Ed mentions that he's driving but it falls on deaf ears as he ushers us through. I glance at the toilet door as we pass, wondering if Jane has fallen in.

Mum will be pleased to know that the living room isn't particularly spacious, and that Jane appears to be a member of the Live, Laugh, Love fan club, something that Mum despises. However, everything is brand new, from the leather suite to the glass coffee table and the fluffy white, oversized lamp shade which matches the fluffy white throw cushions.

'Hi, everyone!'

I drag my eyes away from the cushions to see Jane standing at the door and my jaw hits the floor. She can't be much older than twenty-one and she's wearing low-rise jeans.

'Hi,' I respond. 'Is the loo free?'

I don't wait for a response. Instead, I scurry on out of there and into the bathroom, hoping my jaw retracts by the time I'm finished.

I sit on the loo and put my head in my hands. He's thirty-four and he's dating someone closer to my age. I'm mortified. She looks like Britney Spears. What the hell is he thinking? I mean, maybe he's not *old* old, but he's still too old for her.

When I finally lift my head, I take a moment to look around the bathroom while I finish peeing. White tiled floor, jacuzzi bath and monogrammed his-and-hers towels hanging below the sink. Jesus, there's even a silver love-heart-shaped toothbrush holder.

As tempted as I am to hide in here all afternoon, I've

left Ed alone with them and if I don't go back, he'll make me walk home.

I wash my hands and take a peek inside their bathroom cabinet, which contains the usual paracetamol and ibuprofen, and nothing prescribed by a psychiatrist to indicate that my dad has lost touch with reality. I take a deep breath and return to the living room.

'There she is,' Dad says, his hand already clutching a beer. 'What can I get you?'

Ed's sitting on the couch with a beer to be polite. I know he'll only take a couple of sips and ditch it when no one's looking. Jane is fiddling with one of her earrings while my dad places her wine on the coffee table. I think I might need one of those to get through the afternoon.

'Wine is fine,' I reply, taking a seat beside Ed. 'The flat is lovely, by the way.'

'Penthouse,' he says, giving Jane a nudge. 'I got the last one.'

I smile as he hands me my glass. 'Work must be going well, then?'

'Branch manager,' he replies, plonking himself down beside Jane who still hasn't figured out how her earrings work. 'I'm thinking of going out on my own, though. Something more bespoke, you know? Where the big money is.'

The audacity of this man. I'm one hundred per cent certain that his big salary never equated to bigger child-support payments.

'Anyway, cheers, everyone!' he toasts. 'I got some sandwiches and things from Marks and Sparks for lunch. I'll just bring them through.'

Jane looks a tad apprehensive as he leaves, like I'm about to start interrogating her. Which, of course, is true.

'So are you from Sheffield?' I ask her as she knocks back her wine.

'Loxley,' she replies, nodding. 'You're in Castleton, right? I hear it's lovely.'

Dad reappears with the food, placing the tray on the coffee table.

'It is lovely,' I tell her. 'Maybe Dad will take you there one day. Show you where he grew up.'

'It's dull,' Dad informs her. 'Bugger all to do, unless you like hiking.'

I take a sandwich from the tray. Of course, he wouldn't take her back to Castleton, not after the way he left Mum. The locals would string him up.

'And how did you guys meet?' Ed asks Jane, doing his best to keep the conversation flowing while I eat.

'Funniest story,' she says. 'Brian came into my work looking for a gift for you for passing your exams. I just thought it was the sweetest gesture.'

Ed almost chokes on his beer while I glance at my dad, whose face has suddenly gone very pale. My eyes narrow.

'Sorry, Jane, where is it you work?'

'Yves Saint Laurent counter at Boots,' she replies. 'We spent ages choosing the right thing, didn't we Bri?'

Bri nods. 'Well, you know . . . erm, eat up everyone.'

'Did you like it?' she asks me. 'I love Black Opium. It's so classy.'

'I do,' I reply. 'It was very thoughtful. Dad's like that, right, Dad?'

I take a long swig of my wine. I wonder if he gave the perfume to someone else or just returned it to a different branch of Boots, because I sure as hell didn't receive it.

'Jane, love, keep Ed company while I give Katie a quick tour of the flat.'

'Of course – though excuse the mess in the spare room. I'm trying to sort out my wardrobe.'

I follow Dad down the hall and into the kitchen, where he closes the door behind him. There are several empty beer bottles on the worktop. Looks like he started the party early.

'Look,' he begins. 'I can explain—'

'Explain what? That you lied to her about what a brilliant dad you are, so she'd go out with you? Or explain why I didn't actually receive anything from you for passing my exams. Ed got a bloody car; I didn't even get a card.'

'It wasn't quite like that, but yes, I'm sorry – I should have sent you something. That's why I wanted you over. To celebrate! Your exams, uni, my new flat.'

'Why on earth would I celebrate your new flat?' I ask.

'We've lived in that pokey house for years, with the broken front door and the damp in the bathroom. Maybe you left all that behind, but we didn't. You left us in the shit, so don't fucking expect me to be happy for you.'

'Katie, don't speak to me like that.'

'Six months before you got in touch!' I exclaim. 'You vanished and I didn't hear from you for six months, but I still came to see you because you're my dad. And now we're two years down the line and I rarely hear from you, except for the odd pissed phone call or text message when you remember that I exist!'

'Keep your voice down.'

'Why? In case your girlfriend finds out what a fraud you are? Enjoy the flat, enjoy your booze and your midlife crisis or whatever the hell is going on here. I'm leaving.'

I open the kitchen door and see Ed standing there with my jacket.

'You're just like your mother,' Dad mutters, opening another bottle.

'Well, it's better than being like you,' I reply. 'At least Mum has found someone who won't drink all his money away.'

'Your mum's seeing someone?'

'Bye, Dad.'

Ed follows me out of the flat, into the lift and I manage to make it three floors down before I start to cry. I'm so angry and upset. The absolute nerve of the man.

2010

Kate

'I swear, Gubba, she's about my age. She had a belly ring and everything. He's utterly ridiculous.'

I've lost count of the times I've vented to Gubba in her kitchen. The lemon room with the bright white net curtains and the three weird flying ducks on the wall is my safe space. She's heard it all over the years from school problems, Ed worries, fights with my mum – everything. I'm very lucky to have her.

Gubba clicks on the kettle to make our second pot of tea. She's just had her hair done and it looks really nice – like a little white cloud on top of her head. She stopped colouring it a few years ago and just let her grey hair grow in. I must admit, I miss her red hair. It's funny how the red gene skipped Mum but landed squarely on my head.

'You know your grandpa was your dad's age when I met him. I was a couple of years older than you are now, so it's not that unusual.'

'This is completely different,' I insist. 'Grandpa didn't have a daughter almost the same age!'

'True,' Gubba says, hand on hip. 'It is a little strange, but your dad has always had an eye for the younger ladies. They're probably the only ones who will put up with his nonsense. Does your mum know about Jane?'

I nod. 'She just laughed and called him a cradle snatcher, but she must be angry, surely?'

'Why?'

'You know, being replaced by a younger model . . .'

Gubba pops the tea cosy on the pot and brings it to the table. 'Oh, your mum is tougher than that. Besides, she hasn't been replaced. There's no great love story here. He's just latched on to yet another idiot who finds him charming. It won't last; it never does.'

'I guess so.' I take a Kit Kat and snap it in two. Gubba always has the best biscuits.

'And don't forget, your mother was once that idiot,' she continues. 'I know he's your dad, lovey, and while he might be making more money now, he's no prize. Your mum knows this, and I think he probably does, too. That's why he's trying so hard to impress everyone.'

I dunk my Kit Kat into my tea and sigh.

'I was really angry with him,' I admit. 'I was yelling at him and everything. I mean, he's got this whole new life now, he even took her on holiday to Egypt! I'm pretty certain Mum would have liked Egypt.'

'I'm pretty certain you would have liked Egypt, too,' Gubba replies, rubbing my hand. 'I understand why you're angry. You're allowed to be angry.'

Fighting back the tears, I shrug. 'Redheads and the sun don't mix,' I mutter. 'Might have been nice to have the chance, though. I've never been on a proper holiday.'

'I know, pet.'

'The thing is, I think I'm more sad than angry now,' I tell her as the tears finally start to flow. 'He's thriving without us; he has everything we don't. I felt like he was rubbing my face in it.'

Gubba doesn't respond right away. Instead, she brings me in for a cuddle and allows me to sob.

'It's all very unfair, isn't it, ducky?' she says softly. 'Just because you're eighteen doesn't make it any easier. We don't get to choose our parents, I'm afraid. If we did, I'd have chosen my best friend Elsa Rennie's mum instead of mine. When we were sixteen, she used to let us smoke indoors and would sneak us a bottle of white wine at Christmas.'

I start to laugh. 'That's your definition of good parenting?'

She sips her tea and smiles. 'Oh no. We got away with murder. That's why I'd pick her. My mother was harsh, to put it mildly. She couldn't even tolerate me having friends over.'

Gubba doesn't talk about my great-grandma often

but when she does, the stories she tells are never particularly flattering. Mum said that she was cold and mean-spirited.

'Your dad was nice though, wasn't he?' I ask, feeling marginally less tearful. I tear off a piece of kitchen roll and blow my nose, too lazy to reach for one of the several boxes of tissues placed around the house.

She purses her lips. 'He was a very nice man ... very placid. Loved his garden. He put up with a lot from my mother. Christ, even the fishmonger put up with a lot from my mother. She was notoriously difficult. Your great-grandfather William was just a tad hopeless on his own; he wasn't the sharpest knife in the drawer, shall we say. But his heart was in the right place, and he loved me dearly. That I know.'

'I wish I could be so certain,' I reply. 'Sometimes I do wonder.'

'Oh, your dad loves you,' Gubba assures me, without hesitation. 'Just maybe not quite as much as he loves himself. You might be just eighteen Kate, but your dad is the one with a hell of a lot of growing up to do.'

'Agreed,' I reply. 'Even Ed's got his shit together more than my dad has – and Ed talks to his car!'

She halves the last Kit Kat with me. 'You're very fond of Ed, aren't you?'

'Well, yes. I love him.'

She smiles. 'Just be careful, love. Your mother married

the first boy she fell in love with. Remember, it's a big world out there.'

'Well, you married your first love – that didn't turn out so badly.'

'Me?' Grandpa Tom wasn't my first love, ducky.'

I nearly drop the remaining Kit Kat into my tea. 'What? Then who was?'

'My first love was Joseph Harris when I was seventeen. I worked in his parents' shoe shop, down Cross Street and his mum made him walk me home after my shift so that no one would take advantage of me. She was a kind woman. Fond of the Church.'

She starts to laugh. 'He took advantage of me for six months. His mother had no idea.'

'Gubba!'

'I thought he was the bee's knees. Blond hair, blue eyes, about five ten.'

I'm on the edge of my seat here. 'So, what happened?'

'He joined the Navy and I never saw him again. He wrote a couple of times, but the letters soon stopped. I was heartbroken. I heard years later that he'd married a fellow officer.'

'And then you met Grandpa?'

'I did, and he was the complete opposite of Joe, in all the best ways. All I'm saying is, there's no rush.'

'I know,' I reply. 'You don't need to worry. Marriage and babies could not be further from my mind right now. I have a law degree to complete and a world to change first!'

'That's my girl.'

I finish my tea and kiss Gubba goodbye. I understand where she's coming from. She doesn't want me to settle. And neither do I.

BOXING DAY

Kate

'So what did you say to Tom to make him perk up?' I ask Ed, as we drive out of Hope. I always get a little melancholy when I leave, like I'm leaving a part of me behind.

'I just told him to check his Fortnite skins,' he replies. 'There were some new DLCs he was going on about.'

'Oh, right,' I reply, pretending I understand a word of that. He might as well be speaking Russian. My knowledge of gaming is limited to Candy Crush and Words With Friends.

'He's growing up so fast,' Ed remarks. 'Like, he's grown at least an inch and he's got a proper little-dude haircut.'

I laugh. 'I noticed that! It's cute and also terrifying. Before we know it, he'll be sprouting facial hair and asking us to buy him booze . . . Speaking of booze . . .'

We pull up outside my dad's flat on the outskirts of Sheffield and park next to a car that's been clamped, stripped for parts and spray-painted with the word Scum. Ed looks around nervously.

'This place has got worse,' he remarks. 'That flat wasn't boarded up last time, was it?'

'No,' I reply, feeling uneasy. 'Pretty sure that old fella with the angry cat lived there. Wonder what happened . . .'

We get out and enter the courtyard, climbing the steps to the first floor, then along the landing. I hate this place. It should have been condemned years ago but the council decided it would be the perfect place to house the most vulnerable, most desperate and most likely to re-offend if given half the chance.

I love my dad but he's emotionally draining. He's a forty-five-year-old man, who still thinks he's thirty and is more than partial to an afternoon tipple – or at any time, really.

When he left Mum, he was working for a furniture company in Sheffield and, unsurprisingly, had the gift of the gab when it came to selling beds, sofas and mirrored wardrobes, especially to women. I'm certain his charm and banter were what attracted Mum in the first place, as it certainly wasn't his academic prowess or his hedge fund. Rather quickly, he was promoted to store manager, and within three years, he'd developed relationships, negotiated with suppliers and opened his own store near Bakewell, which people flocked to. Most men would have started laying down some roots at forty, but my dad always wanted more. Wanted better. Better car, better house, better girlfriend, always convinced that there was something more around the corner, waiting for him.

But then Ikea came to town. Ikea with its delicious meatballs and huge car park, its creche and its ability to quickly price my dad right out of the market. He sold the store three years ago but continued to live like he was still the king of occasional tables. It was embarrassing. Last Christmas, we had the pleasure of meeting his current girlfriend, Danielle, who couldn't have been more than twenty-five but even Dad wasn't sure. I'm not sure he bothered to ask.

I got the news in March that he'd been evicted after drinking and partying away six months' worth of mortgage payments. Homeless, he reached out to the council, and they placed him here.

We find number 9 and I knock on the door. Last time we visited, it took him fifteen minutes to open the door as he'd got so pissed the night before, he'd lost his keys. He found them eventually, in the freezer. Thankfully, this time, he opens right away.

'Katie, my love! Eddie! Merry Christmas! Come in, come in!'

I almost take a step back and check I have the right flat. Standing at the door is a clean-shaven, fully suited man who resembles my dad but isn't holding a beer can and wearing a tiger-print robe and one sock.

'Dad?' I say, looking him up and down. 'What the hell happened? I mean you look great but . . . oh shit, are you due in court or something?'

'No,' he replies, with a smirk. 'I just haven't had a drink in eight weeks, is all. Tidied myself up a bit, y'know; clean on the inside, clean on the outside.'

'OK. Sure,' I reply, stepping inside. Ed follows me in and shuts the door behind him, wishing my dad a Merry Christmas. He looks just as confused as I am.

Sadly, the new look doesn't apply to his flat, but I keep my mouth shut as I try to navigate around piles of books, boxes and bin bags in the hallway. God, the air is thick with dust . . . and dog hair. Last time I checked, my dad didn't own a dog.

'Sounds like you're going to meetings again,' I reply, trying not to touch whatever sticky shit is on the living-room door handle. 'Good for you.'

'Yeah,' he replies. 'Three times a week down the West Church. It's been good for me.'

We step into the living room, which is marginally cleaner than the hall but not by much. His sofa looks like it's on its last legs, and again, it's covered in dog hair. I choose to sit at the small table near the window, first removing a pair of stained trousers which look like they wouldn't even survive a wash if offered one.

'No Danielle today?' I ask, already knowing the answer. There's no way her designer shoes would tread anywhere near these carpets. She'll have dumped his arse the moment he lost the penthouse flat with the jacuzzi bath.

'Ah, y'know,' he responds. 'Time to move on.'

'Whose car is that outside, Brian?' Ed asks, peering out the living-room window. 'The burnt-out one?'

'Roland Logan's,' Dad replies. 'Guy who lives in number 20. Or should I say, lived at number 20 until he got lifted. Three am police raid. No idea what for, but from the state of that car, it can't have been good.'

'Shall I put the kettle on,' I ask, getting up. 'You might want a cuppa with your Christmas present.'

'You got me a Christmas present?' he asks. 'I wasn't expecting that. What is it?'

I take the parcel out of my bag and hand it to him. 'Nothing much,' I reply. 'Just a token.'

He unwraps a box of handmade shortbread from the local bakery. It was a staple in our house, growing up.

'I haven't had this in years,' he says, beaming. 'Gertrude at the baker's used to keep a box back for me as it always sold out so quickly.'

That's not all she kept back for you, I think to myself, feeling glad that I don't actually verbalise that really shit sex pun. One of my dad's many short-lived affairs was with Gertrude for two weeks until my mum found out and threatened to have the entire village boycott the store. I'm not sure whether it was that or the dog shit through the letterbox, which caused Gertrude to leave Castleford three weeks later. The baker who owns it now is a man named Miguel and I'm at least sixty-eight per cent certain that my dad hasn't tried it on with him.

The kitchen looks like a bomb has gone off. Empty takeaway boxes are strewn everywhere, the small table is completely covered in coffee rings and food stains and there are food-encrusted dishes in various states of disgusting, all stacked high in the sink. As I struggle to find some clean cups, I realise that while my dad is making progress, he clearly has a long way to go.

I can only find two mugs but there's a six-pack of Coke in the fridge and a bottle of what looks like apple juice but I'm not taking any chances.

'Ed, do you want tea or a Coke?' I yell. 'It's not diet, though.'

Two seconds later he appears at the kitchen door. 'Actually, I thought I'd give you some time alone with your dad.'

'Oh,' I reply, slightly confused. We always visit together. 'So – what? You'll just come back and collect me?'

'Yeah.'

'Right, OK,' I reply. 'What are you going to do while I'm here?'

He sticks one hand in his pocket and rubs his neck. 'Well, actually, I said I'd meet Carly for a drink. Her sister lives not too far from here. Be nice to have a proper catch-up.'

'Carly? When did you arrange that?'

Stay calm Kate, I tell myself. *It's just a drink.*

'She sent me a message this morning. Just a couple of hours; give me a text when you're ready to go.'

Before I can say anything, he's saying bye to my dad and the front door slams shut. I look out of the window and watch him get in the car.

Ed

My satnav directs me to a quiet cul-de-sac about fifteen minutes from Kate's dad's house, although it's like they're on two different planets. There are no burnt-out cars, no graffiti and no smashed-in windows. It's all well-maintained gardens, double glazing and Welcome door mats, so pristine you'd be frightened to wipe your feet on them.

I park up outside number 12 and just as I'm about to get out my phone rings.

'How are ya big man? All going well up in peaky land?'

It's Graham. God, I'm happy to hear his voice, but I control my need to tell him that in case he thinks he's dialled the wrong number and hangs up. As much as we like each other, we're never overtly affectionate, unlike Kate and Lauren who practically explode with delight when they see each other, even if the last time was just five minutes ago. Besides, it's Christmas and I don't intend to vomit my troubles all over him when he's only calling to see if I got a PS5.

'Not bad, mate,' I reply. 'Just dropped Kate at her dad's house, so I'm making myself scarce for a couple of hours. Did you have a nice Christmas?'

'It was all right,' he says. 'Feeling a bit rough today, mind you. Me and Iona ended up at some party in Mala-hide – it was awful and hilarious at the same time. Blokes with no socks on and a sea of fake tan as far as the eye could see. I swear everyone was the colour of a roasted peanut. Well, except me, but I work hard repelling any kind of sunlight.'

'Iona trying to set you up again?' I ask. I've only met his sister once, and from what I can gather she's very fun but rather overprotective of her younger (by three minutes) twin brother.

'Of course,' he replies. 'It'll be me mam's doing. She's got this bee in her bonnet about telling folk I'm divorced, so she's set the twin on me. She'll be calling Father Con-nolly to have a word with me any day now if my sister fails in her mission, which she obviously will if last night is anything to go by. My sister knows a variety of arseholes and I feel like I've failed her somehow.'

Graham Brannigan, my good friend since university and a former history teacher, divorced his wife two years ago, and decided to pursue a career as a stand-up comedian, probably at the lowest point in his life. Turns out the deadpan, Irish, self-deprecating humour his wife hated so much was a huge hit around the comedy clubs of

London. We worked together for three years, and although I haven't seen Graham in a couple of months, I did watch him recently on *Would I Lie to You?* with Bob Mortimer and I haven't laughed so much in ages.

'When are you back in London?' I ask. 'We really need to get a drink soon.'

'New Year,' he replies. 'I've got some stuff on. It's quite nice being home, though, I must admit. How's Kate? She well?'

'Mmm-hmm,' I reply, lying through my teeth. 'All good here . . . Actually, I'm about to visit Carly. You remember Carly?'

He pauses, then laughs. 'Oh my god, Clarinet Carly? How did that come about?'

'Bumped into her on Christmas Eve,' I explain. 'She's visiting her sister.'

'Oh aye? 'Graham replies. 'Just you be careful there. We all know how she lusted after your tall arse at uni. Don't let that Christmas sherry go to your head.'

'What?' I exclaim, genuinely confused by his statement. 'That's nonsense.'

'I'm telling you,' he continues. 'You were too busy with Kate to notice, but you must have been the only one who didn't.'

'Whatever,' I reply, feeling awkward. 'I need to go. I'm sitting in a terrible car in a very nice neighbourhood and I'm certain someone's called the police by now.'

'No problem,' he replies. 'Listen, I'll give you a bell at New Year. Give my love to Kate, the temptress and your arresting officer.'

'Will do. Speak soon, mate.'

Carly's already at the door as I walk up the path, her arms outstretched.

'I'm so glad you made it!' she exclaims, hugging me. 'I was worried you wouldn't have time.'

'Kate's visiting her dad,' I say, following her in. 'And I'd much rather be here, believe me.'

I follow her inside, where she asks me to take my shoes off. 'Bethan's a bit weird about her carpets,' she tells me. 'She likes them more than her husband.'

Bethan and her husband have gone to visit her in-laws for the day, leaving Carly and me to catch up. Her house is pretty sweet, I won't lie, but it's like a show home. Nothing out of place and everything in various shades of stainable. I fear even the piling on my socks might leave an unwelcome trace.

'Tea or coffee?' Carly asks, fishing about in the cupboard for cups. 'They have one of those fancy coffee machines you stick the pods in.'

'Sounds good,' I reply, wondering how Carly's managed to look exactly the same since uni, while I'm beginning to sprout grey hairs in every inconvenient place.

We sit at the kitchen table with a plate of biscuits and catch up, Carly filling me in on what it's like to tour with a professional orchestra, while I divulge what life is like as a high-school teacher.

'You know, I knew you'd end up doing something like that,' she tells me, offering me another biscotti. 'You were always so bloody patient and calm while the rest of us were tearing our hair out. It must be a right laugh working with teenagers.'

'You did just hear my story about the voice break, yeah?'

She laughs. 'Yeah, I'm sure they're little bastards at times, but still. You're making a difference. My music teacher, Mrs Norris, changed my life. One day someone will say that about you.'

I smile. 'Nice thought, but . . . god . . . I dunno. I look at you and I see everything that I didn't do. Does that make sense?'

'Since when did you want to play in an orchestra?' she asks. 'You were never into that side of things. Oh, I saw Ruth in *Hamilton* at the Victoria Palace.'

'God, now I feel worse!' I say. 'Can I bang my head against this nice table if I use a coaster?'

'What?'

'Ugh, it's nothing. Just that you – well, all of you, ended up doing something quite extraordinary. Even Graham is on the telly now. It makes me feel like if you looked up "ordinary" in the dictionary, there would just be a picture of me marking homework.'

'Don't be stupid,' she replies, kicking me under the table. 'More coffee?'

'Sure,' I reply. 'I have time for one more.'

'Whatever happened to that guy you were dating at uni?' I ask, watching her open and close cupboards. 'What was his name? Colin?'

'Keiran,' she replies. 'We split up a month after graduation. He just wasn't for me.'

'Sorry to hear that,' I say.

'Oh, it's fine. My university romances were always short-lived. The annoying thing is that I spent most of uni smitten with someone who was perfect for me. Sadly, I just wasn't perfect for them.'

'No?'

She shakes her head. 'They preferred redheads.'

It takes a second for the penny to drop and when it does, I feel my entire face burst into flames. How did I not see this?

'Carly, I—'

'Don't even sweat it,' she laughs, bringing over the coffee. 'I'm just not lucky in that way. I never have been. Kate seems lovely, she really does. You look happy. You're exactly where you're supposed to be.'

'Maybe,' I reply, not wanting to disclose any information about my situation with Kate. It would be disrespectful, given her insecurities about Carly. 'Who knows what the future holds, right?'

'Right,' Carly agrees. 'Onwards and upwards. Now where does Bethan keep the good biscuits?'

As she raids the cupboards I wonder if she's right. Maybe I am exactly where I'm supposed to be, which, in about six hours, will be completely alone.

Kate

I flick the switch on the kettle and start pacing, my mind going into overdrive with a million questions. She has his number . . . he has *her* number. Do they text often? Do they share emojis and memes and funny little gifs and reminisce about fucking music camp and university and . . .

The kettle clicks off and I take a breath. It's just a drink, Kate, get a hold of yourself.

I take the tea through to the living room where Dad has popped on the fire and cleared a space on the coffee table.

'So, how's things, Katie?' he asks, breaking off some shortbread. 'Have a good Christmas?'

When I was little my dad called me Katie bear, for reasons known only to him. As I got older, he dropped the bear, but I don't think he's ever called me just Kate in my entire life.

'Yeah,' I reply. 'It's been lovely seeing everyone. Tom's getting so big.'

'That's nice,' he replies. Then there is silence, apart from the noise of him slurping his tea.

'Been getting out much?' I ask, knowing that he hasn't. This isn't the home of someone with a social life. There are no friends popping round for coffee or dinner. This house is a reflection of an unhappy life now spent alone. My dad is only forty-five and it breaks my heart.

'Just the meetings,' he answers. 'The shops . . . maybe the odd walk to the park, if it's nice.'

This man used to hit the clubs every weekend and now suddenly he's Gubba? This is too surreal.

The conversation is scarce and stilted. When my dad was drinking, he was hard work but at least he had something to say. I think this is the first visit I've had in years where he's been sober and it's almost like he's disappeared. He hasn't even bothered dying his greys.

'Ed off to meet a friend, then?' he asks. 'Shame he couldn't stay, though I don't blame him. Place is a pigsty. It just gets away from me, you know?'

'So let's do something about it, then,' I say, putting down my tea.

'What?'

I march myself through to the kitchen and throw open the cupboards under the sink.

Bin bags, rubber gloves, bleach, polish, cloths, washing-up liquid . . . I collect it all and dump it on the kitchen table. For a man who never cleans, he has more cleaning products than anyone I know.

'Right, I'm going to start in the kitchen, and you're going to take all that shite in the hall down to the bins.'

'You don't have to do this,' he says. I don't think I've ever seen him look ashamed until now. Funny thing is, I feel exactly the same. It was like this when we visited in April, and I just left him to wallow in it. Regardless of his faults, he's still my dad. What kind of daughter does that make me?

I walk over and hug him. 'Oh, I do have to do this, Dad,' I say, trying not to cry. 'I do because every year I come here, and you're drunk or you're cosying up to some idiot teenager in a pair of ugly Valentino's. Every year I feel angry and reluctant to help because that destructive lifestyle meant more to you than I did.'

I feel him bury his face into my shoulder.

'I thought that showing up here was enough. That I'd done my bit, my due diligence. I thought this was about me – and god knows, I seem to do that a lot.'

I move away so I can see his face. 'Dad, I'm going to help you. And not just by clearing up here. I mean I'm going to really help you – whatever you need.'

'I can't ask you to do that.'

'You didn't,' I reply.

He nods and wipes his eyes with the sleeve of his shirt. 'Better get those bags moved then, eh?'

I smile. 'And put on some music, Dad. It's an absolute crime to have all that vinyl just sitting there.'

He laughs while I take my phone from my bag and send Ed a text.

Going to help Dad clear up a bit, maybe get some dinner with Carly? See you around six.

I'll give Dad his due – he really mucks in, making several trips to the huge communal bins while I get on with cleaning. While most things scrub up rather well, there's stuff that just cannot be salvaged – plates, pots, the toilet seat, bedding – and I make a list as I go of everything that has to be replaced. He also needs a new couch, curtains and a television that wasn't made in 1995.

'You need some plants in here, Dad,' I tell him. 'It'll brighten the room up.'

He laughs. 'Your mum liked plants, too. I remember when she brought home this huge eight-foot palm-tree-looking thing. Far too big; the only place we could have it was by the living-room window, and it blocked out all the bloody light.'

His smile looks bittersweet.

'What happened with you and Mum?' I ask. 'I mean, I know about the affairs but what led to all that?'

He sinks down on to the couch and sighs. 'You know, I've asked myself that question numerous times over the years. We were so young when we got married and, well, we thought it was the right thing to do, you know, with you on the way. But the truth is, we were just never right for each other, Christ, I wouldn't even have called us friends in the beginning. She took to motherhood so quickly and I . . . I was just a scared, stupid lad. I mean, we did our best, but you can't force that kind of connection, you know? Like the one you and Ed have. Anyway, she kicked me out, so I took the car and left. There isn't a day that goes by where I don't regret my actions. I mean, I had to leave – we were all miserable – but leaving you both unprovided for. The shame that comes with that is overwhelming. I'm just grateful you're even talking to me.'

'We all mess up, Dad,' I tell him. 'You have to move on. But just promise me one thing?'

'Yes?'

'When you mess up again, which you will, you tell me, and we'll talk it through.'

He nods. 'I promise.'

'You have a whole other life ahead of you, Dad,' I tell him. 'One with a job, with friends, with love.'

'Maybe with grandchildren?'

I laugh out loud. 'Fucking hell. Is that all anyone thinks about? Listen, Ed will be here soon, let's finish up.' I have no doubt that one day he'll be able to move on from here, but until then, he has somewhere clean and warm to call home.

'Tomorrow I'm going to order you some new stuff, so I'll text you the delivery dates and times. I'm also hiring you a cleaner once a week, until you feel like you're able to cope with all this on your own.'

'This is too much, Katie,' he says. 'I don't know how to thank you.'

'I'll tell you how,' I reply. 'Tomorrow you get an appointment with your GP, and you find out about counselling. And you keep going to your meetings.'

I hear a knock at the front door.

'We have a deal?' I ask.

'We do, love. I won't let you down.'

I hug my dad so hard, I'm afraid I might hurt him. 'I love you. I'll call you in a couple of days.'

I open the front door and see Ed's jaw drop as he looks at the hallway he left just a few hours ago.

'Jesus, I thought I had the wrong flat there,' he says, grinning. 'What a difference.'

'Teamwork,' I tell him, picking up my bag. 'We're off now, Dad. I'll see you soon.'

I close the door behind me and start to cry.

Ed

I have no idea why Kate's crying as we leave her dad's place, and she won't stop sobbing for long enough to tell me. By the time we get into the car, she's calmed down a little, but her sobs still come like little hiccups.

'This might cheer you up,' I say, showing her my phone. She looks at the map open on my screen and starts to cry again.

'What? I thought this was what you wanted? I thought you'd be happy?'

'I'm not a good person, Ed,' she says, wailing. 'I'm selfish and . . . and I'm stubborn and I'm jealous—'

'God, take a breath, Kate.' I hug her, letting her berate herself until she calms down. 'Feel better after all that?' I ask, but she shakes her head, scrambling around for a tissue.

'I just left him there to rot,' she says, wiping her nose on a napkin she's found in the glovebox. 'Every year we go there, and I just look around and think, how can anyone live like this, but he's brought it on himself. Who does that?'

'You're being too hard on yourself,' I tell her. 'And he wasn't in any mindset to accept help from anyone.'

'But I could have tried,' she says softly. 'Fuck, I used to be a good person, Ed. I have no idea when I turned into this work-obsessed, joyless bitch who loses her shit over a fucking phone map!'

'Look,' I say, trying to calm her before she starts crying again. 'First of all, you *are* a good person. No, you're an amazing person – you've just lost your way. You'll get it back.'

'I don't want to end up alone like my dad,' she says quietly. 'He's spent his life wanting more, striving for fuck knows what, and look where it's got him.'

'You're nothing like your dad, Kate,' I reply. 'That I'm sure of.'

'I'm so sorry, Ed. For everything,' she tells me. 'You're my best friend and I'm so grateful I met you.'

'Me too,' I say, passing her another napkin, 'though you might want to deal with that sob snot as I'm finding it really hard not to make fun of you.'

She sniffs and flips down the passenger-side mirror. 'I don't understand how you do it,' she says, cleaning herself up. 'You're still the same person I met in the lunch hall that day. Funny, kind, unshakeable.'

'Handsome,' I interject. 'You forgot handsome.'

'I'm being serious. You know who you are, and you always have. I wasn't bored with that side of you, I was resentful.' She flips the mirror back up.

'You were right when you said I was insecure,' she admits. 'It's a trait I don't like and as I'm discovering, I have many undesirable traits I'd rather not hold on to. Even you just mentioning Carly makes me worried that I'm not good enough.'

'Honestly, we're just—'

'Friends, I know. Ed . . . I don't want to break up.'

'I don't either,' I reply. 'But I think we have to. For a while, anyway.'

She rubs her forehead and exhales.

'Kate, I'm glad you're upset.'

She looks at me like I've just slapped her. 'What?'

I nod. 'I am. I'm happy you're having an existential crisis or a self-reflective breakdown or whatever the hell this is because it means you remember who you are.'

She looks a little less shocked but still wary.

'You were absolutely right when you said that people were supposed to change, but you cannot change what's in your soul and fucking hell, Kate, you have the most beautiful soul. I love you for that.'

I see tears forming again but it's different this time. She takes my hand and wraps her fingers around mine.

'Then I don't understand why we—'

'Because around me, you can't think clearly,' I reply.

'And perhaps I'm the same with you. All I want to do is make you happy, but you're wrong about me. I don't know who *I* am. I only know who I am with you. And maybe that's not enough. Look, I'm not suggesting we start dividing assets or even telling anyone; god knows that's not a conversation I'm ready to have with my parents. I just think some time apart would be for the best. We both need it.'

She lowers her head. 'I'll move into an Airbnb for a bit,' she suggests. 'Just while we figure things out. You stay in the flat, it's closer to your school.'

'You sure?'

She nods.

I let go of her hand and start the car.

2007

Kate

'I don't understand why they're making us do this,' I say to Mum. 'It's like a hillbilly nightmare.'

'Nonsense, it'll be fun!' Mum insists, pulling at the fringing on my skirt. 'You're always complaining that the Christmas discos are lame, maybe this year will be better.'

I highly doubt it. Previous school Christmas discos were completely awful, but at least they weren't playing Country and Western music and making us dress up like bloody cowboys. A Christmas hoedown. Really? I need to find a new school.

'I bet this was Lindsay Templeton's mum's idea,' I say, glaring at myself in the mirror. 'She's on the parent council, she always wears denim and they live on a farm. Guaranteed she came up with this.'

Mum smiles. 'I wouldn't call a few chickens a farm, but you might be right. I've heard she's quite active on the committee. One of the reasons I'm not. There . . . All done.'

She stands to the side while I slowly die inside. Never

in my fifteen years on earth did I think I'd be wearing a fringed denim skirt, a blue plaid shirt tied at the waist and cowboy boots.

'Your hair looks so cute!' Mum squeals. 'Are you sure you don't want to wear the cowboy hat? You suit hats.'

I'll admit that my hair does look kind of cute. Two chunky plaits, with little loose curls down either side. 'No to the hat,' I insist. 'I think the skirt fringing and the gun holster are more than enough humiliation for one evening.'

I hear a loud knock on the door downstairs. 'Gubba,' I yell. 'Can you let Ed in?'

Mum fusses with the fringing again until I physically shoo her away.

'Ed's picking you up for the dance?' she asks, raising an eyebrow. 'How very gentlemanly of him . . .'

Oh god, there's that look. I wish she wouldn't do that. It's so embarrassing.

'Mum, he always comes in for me on the way to school. This is no different, so you can stop with the suspicious eyebrows. There's no gossip here.'

'I was only asking,' she replies, now smirking. 'I mean, you do spend a lot of time together, I was—'

'I'm leaving now,' I say, feeling my face start to burn which only makes her presume she's correct. Which she isn't. We are not a *we*. Not that I wouldn't like to be a *we*, but Ed's never given me any sign that he likes me in that way. Besides, I'm certain he likes Jenny Parker. Lauren said she passed him a note in class and then she saw her coming out of his house. If I ever get murdered, I want Lauren to investigate.

I head downstairs and see Ed standing with Gubba, smiling politely as she tells him about a school dance she attended four hundred years ago. I start to giggle.

'Don't you laugh,' Ed warns, trying to keep a straight face. 'I already want to throw myself into the River Styx.'

'That shirt!' I exclaim. 'It's hideous! It's perfect! Where did you find it?'

Ed's wearing a brown shirt with huge white flowers on the shoulders and white fringing running from the shoulders to the chest, tucked into his jeans which look just a little too tight.

'Charity shop in Sheffield,' he replies, suddenly looking happier with himself. 'Six quid to look this stupid. Bargain.'

'I was just telling Ed about the time we had our school dance in the village square,' Gubba interjects. 'Impossible trying to feel up your honey, with half the parents and the vicar looking on.'

Mum comes down the stairs behind me. She's still smiling like she knows something I don't.

'OK, well, we're going now,' I say, grabbing Ed by the shirt. 'See you later.'

'Have fun!' Mum shouts as I close the door behind us.

'Sorry about my Gubba,' I say. 'She can be a tad inappropriate after a sherry or two.'

'It's fine,' Ed replies. 'Though I think you should be apologising for that skirt.'

I laugh. 'Says the man in light blue cowboy boots! Did you steal them from the Village People?'

'Yeah, well you look like you'd start a bar fight,' Ed continues as we turn the corner. 'Those pretty pigtails don't fool me.'

'I think you mean purdy pigtails,' I correct. 'And I'm actually really annoyed that you have a gun in your holster, and I don't.'

He grins. 'I'd lend you it, but it's stuck in there unfortunately. Must be in case I pretend to hold up a bank.'

'You realise this is going to be horrible,' I tell Ed as we near the school. 'My worst nightmare is that we're the only ones that show up in full costume.'

'My worst nightmare is that I actually enjoy it,' he replies, and I start to laugh. Apart from Lauren, he's the only person on earth who can make me properly belly laugh. And we have this thing where we make fun of each other to see who can make the other laugh the loudest. I've known Ed for a year now, but it feels like I've known him forever.

Lauren's been paired with William Schofield, and I doubt very much they're arriving together considering he insists on calling her Lauren the lesbo and she, in turn, calls him Billy Bitch-Tits. I'm so glad Ed joined our school; lord knows who I'd have ended up with otherwise.

We can hear the music as we walk into the school grounds. 'Jingle Bell Rock', one of the songs they had us practise to for a fortnight and I officially hate it now. I see other pupils from year 11 ahead of us and I'm instantly relieved that we're not the only ones dressed like idiots.

'You ready to step-touch?' Ed asks, his boots scuffing along the ground.

'Hell, no,' I reply. 'But I think you're secretly looking forward to this.'

He shrugs. 'Might be all right; you never know.'

It's obvious Ed has never been to one of *our* school dances or he'd know they're never all right. We have three every year: Valentine's, Christmas and the end of the school year. I hope to god Lindsay Templeton's mum has been exiled from the PTA by the time Valentine's comes around. God knows what she'd suggest for that.

Ed

The first thing I notice when we enter the gym hall is the hay. There are bales of it all around the edge of the hall and people are sitting awkwardly on them. Then the bunting. Stars and stripes bunting hung from corner to corner over the dancefloor, which so far is empty because everyone is too busy picking straw out of their backsides.

'Yee-haw bitches!' I hear a voice yell behind me. 'Can you believe this shit?'

I turn around to see Lauren, already hugging Kate. Lauren is probably the only other girl I actually like at this school and don't just tolerate for the sake of being friendly. She's quite similar to Kate in some ways but wildly different in others.

'I was going to give the award to Ed for best cowboy, but I think you might have cinched it,' Kate tells her. I'd have to agree. Lauren has dyed her fringe red, white and blue and is wearing a pair of white cow-print trousers with a matching waistcoat. She's also wearing a white cowboy hat which earns her bonus points.

'Ah, thanks,' she replies. 'I thought I'd make an effort since there's feck all else to do around here. I did see several sixth-formers in Daisy Dukes, so I'm hoping they'll get thrown out for corrupting the juniors.'

'Daisy Dukes?' I ask.

Kate points towards the doors where three girls stand in very short denim shorts and belly tops. 'Ah,' I reply, trying not to stare. It's difficult, however. I'm fifteen.

'Where's your dance partner?' I ask Lauren, moving the conversation away from tiny shorts. 'Warming up outside?'

'Billy Bitch-Tits? No idea,' she replies. 'Hopefully, he'll give this one a miss and make my night. The boy smells like hot dogs.'

'Everyone, we're about to begin. Please take to the floor for a warm-up "Cotton Eye Joe".'

Lauren immediately launches herself towards the centre of the room while Kate and I reluctantly follow behind. If it wasn't for Kate, this night would be miserable. In fact, if it wasn't for Kate, my entire existence would be miserable. We reach the dancefloor and the music starts. Not one of us can remember what the hell we're doing. It's an utter shambles, so much so that a couple of teachers have to come to the front to remind us how it's done.

'Having fun yet?' Kate asks, as we bump into each other.

'Nope,' I reply, trying to remember my left from my right. 'But it looks like Lauren is!'

Kate looks over to see Lauren absolutely nailing the line dance, complete with whooping and hollering. She laughs and crashes into me again, almost falling, but I catch her.

'I lied,' I tell her, grinning. 'I'm having the best time ever.'

An hour later and we're all taking a break. Unfortunately for Lauren, William Schofield has turned up and the next dance is couples only.

'Why does god hate me?' Lauren grumbles, watching him unenthusiastically drag himself over. 'I hope he's at least showered.'

Kate and I take our places, ready for the main dance that's been drilled into us for the past two weeks. 'Step into Christmas' begins to play.

It starts off a tad wobbly, with both of us trying to keep up with the beat. But by the time I've spun Kate around for the first time, laughter takes over and we just go with it. We two step, grapevine, make lasso arms and generally look like fools, which I think was the sole intention of whoever organised this event. Weirdly enough, Lauren and William are also laughing and not at each other. It's rather unnerving.

I feel almost giddy on the walk home and far more dishevelled than I was going in. My shirt is now hanging loose, my hair a mess and my boots have rubbed blisters into my heels. Kate looks just as pretty as she always does. She's babbling on about Lauren and William when I decide to do something either extremely brave or really, really stupid.

'Would you like to go out with me?' I ask. God, voice, please don't crack. Not now.

'Sure, where?' she replies. 'Not that café in Bakewell again, though – the owner hates anyone under fifty.'

'No, I mean, like out out. As in, on a date?'

She stops walking. 'Me? But I thought you liked Jenny Parker?'

'Jenny? No. Why would you think that?'

I see Kate's cheeks begin to redden. 'It's just Lauren saw you passing notes and I know she's been to your house and—'

I snort. 'Mum's teaching her piano. She was passing me a cheque to give to her.'

'Well, I feel like an idiot,' Kate confesses. 'I just . . . I never thought that you liked me in that way.'

'I do,' I respond. 'I think you're really nice.' *Really nice? Jesus, Ed, Mr Renton in physics is really nice! Say something else.* 'Hot,' I blurt out. 'I think you're hot.' Fuck, now I'm blushing. If she says no, I'm never doing this again. With anyone. Ever.

Thankfully, her face breaks into a huge smile. 'I think you're hot, too.'

She leans in to kiss me and I swear I've never felt so

excited and terrified at the same time. Her lips are really soft. Wait, is this a yes?

A few seconds later she stops suddenly.

'Sorry, did I do something?'

'Ed, um . . . is that your gun?'

She pulls back a little and I follow her gaze down towards my jeans.

'Yes!' I exclaim, moving my gun holster back to the side. 'Awkward!'

She takes my hand and we walk home laughing, reaching Kate's house first.

'Can I ask you something?' she says, getting her keys from her bag.

'Sure.'

'That wasn't your gun, was it?'

I scrunch up my face. 'Um . . . no. Sorry.'

'Good to know,' she replies, before launching herself on me again.

Oh my god, this is the best night of my life.

DECEMBER 31ST

Kate

'Dancing? Are you kidding me?'

'But it's New Year's Eve,' Lauren replies, like I'm not acutely aware of the day. 'You always go dancing. *We* always go dancing.'

She starts to shimmy in her chair as she lights a cigarette. I've been living with Lauren since I got back from Castleton, as my Airbnb won't be available for another week. So for now, I have to put up with her chair antics and 6am shower singing.

'Yes,' I reply. 'We do go dancing . . . with Ed.'

'So this year, you'll be travelling light,' she answers. 'It's fine. Also, I think it's exactly what you need. Booze, good tunes—'

'Surrounded by couples. No one to kiss at midnight . . .'

'I'll kiss you,' she replies. 'As long as you don't wear that horrible lip gloss you're so fond of, I've seen the way your hair sticks to it. That stuff's like Gorilla Glue.'

'Tempting, but I think I'll pass,' I say. 'Besides, you'll have Dave. I'll be a third wheel. No thank you.'

'Nope, I'm afraid to say that Dave is no longer with us.'

'What? Oh my god, what happened?'

'Oh relax, he's not dead or anything, I just chucked him. There's only so much football I can tolerate. I swear he was more interested in looking at my 75-inch TV than at me.'

I'm reminded that my future Airbnb only has a piti-ful 32-inch television and feel that Dave may have been wrongfully and unfairly dismissed.

'Have a look through my wardrobe,' she suggests. 'Or I can drive over and pick some stuff up for you?'

'No need. Besides, I have to pop in to a client's little gathering at seven,' I tell her. 'I'd rather not, but my boss is insisting I go to scout for potential clients. I mean, seri-ously – does she want me to break up a marriage and then have them hire me? It'll be an hour at the most and then I'm coming back here to watch *Top of the Pops* from 1978.'

'OK, Boomer,' Lauren replies. 'Who's the client? Anyone interesting?'

'Their divorce isn't public yet; you know I can't discuss the—'

'NAME PLEASE.'

'Jesus, it's Tara Mitchell-Brown. Stop yelling.'

'Are you kidding? She's a train wreck, I frickin' love her. I'm so coming with you. I can totally pop in for drinkies and a snoop around her house.'

'No way,' I reply. 'I can't just bring my friends along; that would be highly unprofessional. A partner, maybe, but not a friend.'

'You're not just bringing your friend along; you're bringing your award-winning hairdresser friend along. You know fuck all about the world of celebrity. I can guarantee that this girl knows me. You'll impress the shit out of her and all her soon-to-be-divorced friends. Think of it as networking.'

She's absolutely right, of course. I never thought of that. To me, Lauren is just my best mate, the girl with the cool school shoes who helped me through my parents' divorce and never once complained when I saw less of her to see more of Ed. She's a big deal to me. But I forget that she's also a big deal to a lot of other people, too.

'OK, fine,' I tell her. 'But best behaviour, please.'

A silence falls on her side of the couch. 'Lauren . . .'

'Yep, yep, best behaviour. Brownies' honour.'

'You were thrown out of the Brownies.'

'Good talk,' she says. 'I'll use the shower first.'

She hands me her ciggy and leaves before I can change my mind.

If Tara hadn't sent that invite into work, then Harriet wouldn't have seen it first and I could have made up an excuse so I didn't have to go. This thing with Ed is still raw. I've only been gone four days, but it feels much longer. We've never spent New Year's Eve apart. How can I welcome in a new year without him?

Ed

When I see Graham's number appear on my phone, I'm tempted not to answer it. He's called me four times already and I'm not up for having the same conversation for a fifth time. But if I don't answer it, he'll just keep calling. God, he's annoying.

'For the millionth time, I'm really not in the mood for a party!' I yell, before he even has the chance to say hello. 'I'm just going to have a few beers and watch Jools Holland or something.'

'Wrong,' he replies. 'Because that would mean I have to attend this bloody get-together alone and that's just not an option.'

Graham's been invited to a New Year's Eve party for 'drinks and nibbles' and he's been bugging me to go with him for the past week. I told him that Kate's gone to a spa with her friend because I'm not ready to admit to myself that we've split up, never mind to anyone else.

'I mean, there is the option of not going at all,' I suggest. 'Like I intend to. Just a thought.'

'I have to,' he whines. 'My agent is forcing me to go and be nice to her other clients. I imagine she's going to force them to be nice to me, too, and it's going to be dreadful.'

'Dolly? I can't imagine her forcing you to do anything. She doesn't seem the type. Besides, she'll be there, so you won't be alone.'

Graham's agent, Dolly Latimer, is an absolute legend and one of the nicest people I've ever met; unlike his first agent, Jeremy Winter, who was the manifestation of human slime.

'Don't you be fooled by that woman,' he tells me. 'With her kind face and her fancy glasses ... she's absolutely ruthless when she needs to be. She'll get you to do whatever she wants. She'll just do it in a way that's quite gentle and supportive, and somehow you end up thinking it was your idea.'

'Wow,' I reply. 'Gentle and supportive. What a monster.'

'I know,' he replies. 'And I pay her thirty per cent for the privilege.'

'Thirty?' I question. 'I thought fifteen was the standard.'

'It is!' he exclaims. 'Somehow, I ended up offering her thirty. I told you. Devil woman. So you have to come – for just an hour or two, I promise. Free beer. Look, you have a few days without Kate, come and babysit me.'

'Two hours and then I'm out of there,' I reply. 'Deal?

And don't make me speak to anyone. I'm too tired for small talk.'

'Deal! Meet me at Sloane Square about seven? You're a good man, Edward, so you are. The good lord broke the mould when he—'

'Oh, shut up. I'll see you at seven.'

Kate

We take an Uber to Tara's home in Chelsea, which looks exactly like the pictures I've seen online. A 5-million-pound, four-bedroom terraced house, with a cute blue door on a beautifully clean street lined with Teslas and Mercedes.

'Five mill for this?' Lauren remarks as she peers out of the window. 'If I had five million, I'm not sure I'd be living in a terraced house.'

'London, though, innit?' the Uber driver remarks. 'Crazy money. Happy New Year, ladies.'

We thank him and step out on to the street. I have to agree with Lauren, for £5m I'd buy somewhere in the countryside, with lots of space for my three rescue dogs (Rickman, Bobo and Waffle) to run around. Not that I've thought about it. I certainly wouldn't want to be squashed in like sardines.

I ring the bell at number 7 and wait, aware that I'm being viewed in whatever CCTV they have installed and resisting the urge to wave at the camera like an idiot. I turn to see Lauren craning her neck to try and look in the window.

Before I can rein her back in the door opens and Tara appears. 'Come in, pet,' she says. 'I'm so glad you came.'

'Hi, Tara,' I reply. 'Thanks for asking me. This is my friend Lauren.'

'Nice to meet you,' she says. 'You look familiar, have we met?'

'No,' Lauren replies. 'I'd definitely have remembered!'

She invites us in, and we make it about three steps before I hear Tara gasp. 'Lauren Alexander! I can't believe it!'

'Told you,' whispers Lauren, as she turns around and smiles at Tara.

'Kate, you never mentioned you were mates with Lauren,' Tara says. 'Oh my god, come through and meet everyone. My pal Josie's gonna have a fit when she sees you.'

And with that, Lauren is ushered away, and I can relax a little, though, from the looks of things I am completely underdressed. Tara is wearing a bloody evening gown and here I am in leather trousers and a nice top. Even Lauren's wearing a plain black satin slip dress (albeit with cherry Doc Marten boots); but she is skinny with rose-gold hair. She could wear a prison jumpsuit and still look good.

I grab a glass of fizz from a tiny woman with a tray as I enter the living room. My god, this place is like the Tardis.

The ceilings must be at least sixteen feet high. The décor's a little different from the photos I've seen previously. The white sofas have been replaced by dark brown and the glass coffee table is gone, a chestnut apothecary-style table in its place. I assume this is all far more child friendly, but I actually prefer it. It has personality, rather than an obvious price tag. There is a huge chandelier hanging from the ceiling and a white piano in the corner of the room, but it is Chelsea, after all.

There must be around thirty people here already and not many I recognise. I'm glad that Harriet isn't here, as she'd have expected me to give her *Quantico*-level behaviour profiling on each and every one of them, like I know anything about their lives. To be honest, I imagined walking into a room full of people, all dressed in whatever designer is on trend right now and TikTokking their every move. I'm drawn towards a woman in her early fifties wearing a black evening dress and amazing red sparkly glasses. Once she stops talking on her phone, I'm totally going to make friends with her.

There's an open glass door to the right of me, which leads to the kitchen and I casually wander in to see if the marble island is as beautiful as it is in the photos. I spend very little time in the kitchen, so I'm not sure where my obsession with these islands comes from. Perhaps if I had one, I'd be obsessing over something else, like peekaboo pantries or flagstone floor tiles and . . .

She has flagstone floor tiles. Of course she does.

The island is just as striking as I thought it would be, with three silver breakfast-bar stools on one side facing a glass electric hob on the other.

'Can I help you with anything?'

My eyes dart towards the voice and I wince. There are at least six people in the kitchen, but they're not guests. They're catering staff and have been watching me skulk around the island for the past couple of minutes. God, I think I audibly *oohed* at one point.

'Oh, no. Thanks,' I reply and smile politely as I back out of the room, trying not to get in their way. The last time Ed and I threw a party (guest list of twelve), there were always people hanging out in the kitchen, despite its size. People congregate in kitchens – it's human nature; but I guess when you've hired waiting staff, there's no need for guests to be in there.

Back in the living room, I see Lauren in a corner of the room, chatting to Tara and a few others. She's obviously far more comfortable in this setting than I am but that doesn't surprise me. Lauren just adapts to her surroundings, like a chameleon. Even as a teenager she would just show up and fit right in, regardless of where we were. She has never once questioned who she is and it shows, whereas my self-esteem is still a work in progress. I love that for her, and I hate it for me.

I walk over to a woman in gold, standing by the fireplace and introduce myself.

'Ah, the lawyer!' she says, air-kissing me. 'Jade Hart. Tara's been telling me all about you!'

For someone who doesn't want their divorce made public, Tara's certainly not keeping it quiet.

'All good, I hope,' I reply, like a big walking cliché. 'So how do you know Tara?'

'Our husbands play for the same team,' she replies, looking at me like I've just stepped off an alien spacecraft. 'Noel Hart . . . over there by the window . . . he's my husband.'

As I look over, my brain suddenly sparks into action. Noel Hart. I know him. Bad hair plugs. Rumours of infidelity with the nanny. Is his face always that red?

'Of course!' I reply. 'So sorry, Jade. You just look a little different from your photos. Have you changed your hair colour?'

'I have,' she replies. 'Darkened my blonde for winter.'

Oh, thank god – I was just pulling ideas out of my arse.

'That'll be it,' I say. 'It makes you look younger. Brings out your eyes.'

'Really? I wasn't sure about it. Thought it was maybe a little too dark?'

The smile radiating from Jade's face tells me that I've successfully managed to avoid looking like a moron, and also that I know more about celebrity culture than I thought. Go, me!

'Have you met my friend, Lauren?' I ask, gesturing towards the back of the room. Lauren's currently knocking back what looks like vodka jelly.

She shakes her head. 'We just arrived. I'm only standing here to heat up. I might as well be naked for all the warmth this dress provides.'

I'm not surprised. She's wearing a gold leopard print mini dress and has zero body fat. I, on the other hand, am about to start sweating profusely if I don't get away from this fire.

'Well, Lauren does hair,' I continue. 'She's amazing. Owns a salon in Kensington with that make-up artist from YouTube – blue hair . . . gosh, what's his name?'

'Jamie King? Wait – your friend is Lauren Alexander?'

'Best friend actually,' I flex. God, I hate myself.

Jade about turns and practically drags me by the arm towards Lauren, like she's being pulled by a tractor beam, loudly introducing me to everyone on the other side of the room as 'Tara's badass lawyer' which, to be fair, is more than Tara has done.

'You bet she is,' Lauren asserts. 'I'm telling you ladies, this is the smartest woman I know and also the greatest. You should totally take her card.'

'No! It's a party! I'm not even sure I brought any with me,' I respond, knowing full well that I have at least twenty bespoke business cards in my bag. I breathe a small sigh of relief. At least I'll hopefully have something positive to share with Harriet when I get back to the office next week.

Half an hour in and I realise I haven't thought about Ed since I got here. Of course, I only realise this by thinking about him, and now I can't stop. I knew there would be couples here, but it's starting to sink in that Ed and I may never be at a party together again. Any married friends we have will have to choose between us and it's likely they'll choose Ed, as he's probably more fun to be around.

'Drink up!' I hear Tara say as she hands me another wine. 'My girls are at their granny's and I intend to enjoy myself. Come on – you're not on the clock you know!'

'Oh, I know,' I reply. 'I've just been chatting too much. Tell me, who's that woman in the red glasses?'

'My agent,' Tara replies. 'Absolute star, though she's crafty as hell. Quite a few folk here are with her talent agency. This party was her idea. Oh, you should meet her. Dolly! DOLLY! Come and meet Kate . . .'

Ed

I hang up and check my watch. It's 5pm already and I'm still in the joggers I wore to bed last night ... and the night before.

I run the shower and spend at least ten minutes debating whether to even get in. I truly cannot be bothered with this. The whole routine of getting showered and changed just to stand in a room full of strangers. And it's New Year's Eve. My first one without Kate. All I want to do is spend it with her. It's been four days since she left and I feel numb. Most of her things are still here, so it feels like she is, too. I have to believe she'll be back; the alternative is too grim to contemplate.

By six-thirty, I'm ready to go, wearing the same shirt I wore on Christmas Day and hoping it doesn't smell. Normally I'd have a bit of a preen before I go out, but I barely even check the mirror. There's no point. I don't give a shit how I look – and besides, there's no one to look nice for, anyway. Looking nice for Kate was never a problem because she'd get excited by the strangest things. I could be wearing designer gear and she'd be more turned on by my hands or even just a look I'd give her. Once she even dragged me into bed when my hair sat a particular way. God, I loved that.

The Tube is unsurprisingly rammed this evening and I find myself uncomfortably squished up against the doors. I'm always slightly in awe of people who can just stand in the carriage, barely holding on to anything and never stumble or fall into someone else when the train suddenly jerks. I certainly wasn't blessed with this skill, knocking my head off the doors several times. I'm not opposed to a concussion right now, to be fair – anything to get out of tonight.

Being six foot three, my height makes it easier to spot Graham when I arrive at a rather crowded Sloane Square. Well, that and the fact he's the only one around who looks like Tom Hanks in *Castaway* from the neck up.

'All right, fella,' he says, looking me up and down. 'I see you're letting the world know you have no intention of having any fun tonight.'

I can't help but laugh. 'The audacity!' I exclaim. 'When you've come out dressed as a malnourished Hagrid.'

'Funny!' he replies. 'Maybe there's hope for you yet.'

'You seem to forget that you also didn't want to come,' I remind him. 'No idea why you're now so chipper.'

'Because I'm spending New Year's Eve with you,' he

replies. 'Oh, listen – I've brought a bottle of whisky with me, because it's horrible and also looks more expensive than it is. If anyone offers you this, say no.'

'I hate whisky, anyway,' I reply. 'Shit, should I have brought anything?'

'Only your big-boy pants!' he replies. 'I doubt Kate's away at her spa retreat pining for you. She'll be covered in cucumber, getting her eyebrows tattooed on or something.'

The house is a twenty-minute walk from the Tube station, which isn't particularly fun when it's minus two, but we have zero chance of catching a cab right now. By seven-thirty, we've finally found the street.

'Shit, let me just call Dolly and get the number?' Graham says. 'I can't find the invite.'

I wait, slowly losing the feeling in my legs, while he swipes down his contacts.

'Dolly, what number is this place? Seven, OK. We'll be there in two secs . . . yes, I did bring a friend – you think I'm hanging out with you all night? Love you, too.'

'Number seven, blue door,' he informs me. 'It sounds quite lively in there. Hopefully, everyone's already drunk and we can pretend we stayed longer than we actually do.

'Sounds like a plan,' I reply, following him towards the house with the blue door. God, I hope this is painless.

Kate

'Oh, here's my boy. Graham, sweetheart! Over here.'

I turn in the direction of Dolly's wildly waving arm and feel my jaw hit the floor. That's Graham. Ed's Graham. Shit . . . wait. Is that Ed?'

Graham waves back then pauses when he sees me. He turns and looks at Ed, who doesn't notice Graham because he's too busy looking at me. What the hell is going on? Why are they here? My head spins around to find Lauren, but she's nowhere to be seen.

'Kate?' Graham asks on approach. 'Wow! Didn't expect to see you here. I thought you were on some spa break with your friend?'

Initially confused, I glance momentarily at Ed and his rapidly greying face before it all makes sense. He hasn't told Graham yet.

'I was,' I reply. 'But the place had to close. Burst pipes or something.'

He still looks confused. 'And you didn't tell Ed you were still in London?'

Oh, screw you and your perfectly logical question, Graham. 'Didn't I? Sorry, Ed. I thought I had.'

'It's fine,' he replies, quickly. 'I mean, burst pipes are common at this time of year.'

'It is common,' Graham agrees, his eyes darting between the pair of us. 'And so is spending New Year with your partner when you're in the same city.'

'Graham – come and meet Tara,' Dolly suggests. 'You can give her your bottle of whatever the hell that is.'

Dolly leads Graham away, leaving Ed and me alone – well, as alone as you can be in a living room jam-packed with party guests. He looks good. Better than I'd hoped he would.

'Well, isn't this awkward?' I say, trying to keep my voice down. Ed grabs a glass of Prosecco and downs it in one. 'If I'd known that your mate Graham shared an agent with Tara . . .'

'Tara? Oh, the Geordie divorce case,' he mutters. 'Of course. Look, I had no idea either, I was just helping Graham out by coming here.'

'But why haven't you told him?' I ask. 'Lauren's here and she knows we've split.'

'You tell Lauren when you sneeze, Kate. Graham and I aren't like that. I'll tell people when I'm ready.'

'Well, you'd better tell him something because now I

look like a weirdo. He probably thinks that I made up the spa thing to cheat on you. I refuse to look like the bad guy here, Ed.'

'I knew I should have stayed in tonight,' he replies. 'What a shitshow.'

'Same,' I reply. 'I didn't want to come here either. Look, I've been here for a while. Maybe I should just make my excuses and leave.'

'No, I should,' he replies. 'Enjoy your—'

'Ed? What the hell are you doing here?'

'Lauren,' he says, spinning around to face her. 'Hey. Yeah, weird coincidence, eh? Turns out my friend Graham shares an agent with Tara.'

'Graham's here?'

'He is and he doesn't know that Ed and I are taking some time apart, so—'

'Well, now I do.'

'Graham!' I yelp in surprise. Jesus, where did he appear from? 'Graham, you remember Lauren, right?'

They say hi to each other before turning their attention back to us. Ed rubs the back of his neck, looking like he just wants to disappear.

'Graham,' I begin, 'Ed and I . . . had a little falling out. I decided to spend a few days with Lauren to let us both cool off.'

I swear if Lauren says anything to the contrary, I'll rugby tackle her. Thankfully, she plays along.

'Obviously, Ed was too embarrassed to tell you the reason why, but I'm sure he'll fill you in.'

Ed's eyes narrow ever so slightly. I can tell he's inwardly cursing me.

Graham laughs. 'And you both ended up at the same party? How unfortunate is that!'

Lauren laughs and Graham looks rather pleased with himself. Wait, are they making flirty eyes at each other? I've seen that look on Lauren's face and it usually ends up with me getting a taxi home alone.

'Anyway,' I say, standing in between the two of them, 'Lauren and I are leaving soon. Have a nice night. Happy New Year.'

'I'm not leaving,' Lauren laughs. 'This is a blast.'

A server appears with a tray full of tequila shots, closely followed by Tara, who's now wearing some tinsel on her head.

'Drink up, everyone!' she demands. 'Youse are all far too sober for my liking!'

The tipsier Tara gets, the stronger her accent becomes. I can tell she's tried to soften it over time, but this is far more endearing. We all take a shot at our host's request.

'Who's this bonny lad?' she asks, looking at Ed. 'Tall one, aren't ya?'

'Ed,' he replies, holding out his hand. 'I'm a friend of Graham's.'

'Well, you're very welcome, Ed. Oh, Kate, you must

come and meet me friend Peter. I know you're not working tonight but his wife just left him for someone off *EastEnders*.'

Lauren chuckles as Tara links arms with me, drags me out of the living room and into a second lounge area, where I'm introduced to a man in a dark grey suit, just as the tequila begins to kick in.

'Kate, this is me friend Pete, a fellow Geordie. He's a producer on the show. Peter, this is Kate.'

Peter looks more than a little drunk.

'Nice to meet you,' I say.

'A fellow ginge!' he says, looking genuinely pleased. 'I like you already.'

'She's helping me with my issue,' Tara says. 'You know, the thing we were talking about. She could help you.'

Peter stares blankly.

'My divorce,' she mouths silently.

'Muddy floors?'

'Jesus, Peter, do I have to hum the *EastEnders* theme tune?'

The penny suddenly drops. 'Ah, shit, yes,' he replies, getting flustered.

I reach into my bag. 'So nice to meet you,' I say, handing him my card. 'If you need some advice, feel free to give me a call – but for now, I say we do shots and get mortal.'

'Mortal!' he exclaims. 'I love this woman!'

Tara screams with laughter and goes to find the nearest server, while I inwardly congratulate myself for successfully googling the Geordie term for drunk in the bathroom.

Ed

'How could I have possibly known that she'd be here?' Graham asks, grabbing another canapé off a passing tray. 'In the years we've known each other, have you ever witnessed any psychic behaviour from me?'

'No,' I reply. 'But I wasn't implying that you were somehow paranormal – it's just far too weird that we'd both end up here.'

'Not really,' he says. 'Agents, lawyers, hairdressers . . . they all run in the same circles. London's really not that big.'

I don't think I've ever heard a more inaccurate statement in my life. 'How much have you had to drink?' I ask him.

'Not nearly enough,' he replies. 'So . . . is she single, then?'

'Who?' I ask, following his gaze.

'Lauren. She has such lovely hair. What colour would you say that is? Pink? Peach?'

'Lauren? Wait – do you fancy Kate's mate?'

'Intrigued, is more the word I'd use,' he replies. 'Captivated. But yeah. I fancy her. She's like a little Easter Egg.'

I look at Lauren again and I'm stunned to see her smiling back at Graham. Never in a million years did I think those two would be remotely attracted to each other. Lauren's all tattoos, vivacious and uninhibited while Graham is gentle, likes reading and has worn the same pair of jeans since I've known him.

'I think she was seeing someone,' I tell him. 'But from the way she's checking you out, I might be mistaken. I say go for it.'

He doesn't need to be told twice and makes a beeline across the room. The night is just getting weirder and weirder.

Looking around, I'm absolutely certain that, apart from the catering staff and Kate, I'm the only person here with a normal job. Everyone else is either on telly or works in telly, whereas I only own a telly. I've never been in the same place as so many well-known people, most of whom are really down to earth. Well, except Noel Hart who just grunted at me. He's a shit centre-forward anyway.

'Jack and Coke?'

I turn to my right and see a woman with thick black eyeliner holding out a glass. She looks familiar but not familiar enough to be offering me a drink. I almost check behind me to make sure there's no one else there, like when you wave at someone only to find they weren't waving at you in the first place.

'Sorry, are you talking to me?'

She laughs. 'Yes, silly. I'm—'

'Holy shit, you're Ashleigh Mason.'

Ashleigh Mason is a singer–songwriter who just won her third Brit Award and is somehow now offering me a drink. My immediate reaction is to look for Kate. Kate adores her.

'And you are . . .'

'Um, Ed,' I reply, still scanning the room. No sign of Kate. She must still be with Tara.

'Is something wrong?' she asks. 'I feel like I'm disturbing you.'

'God, no, I'm sorry,' I say, accepting the drink. 'I don't mean to be rude; I was just looking for my girlfriend. She's a huge fan of yours.'

'And there's me thinking you were all by yourself over here. I hate to see anyone sitting alone. What's your girlfriend's name? I'd love to say hi.'

My girlfriend. It suddenly hits me that she's not my girlfriend anymore. I feel like I've been punched in the guts; but I'm not about to clarify the situation to Ashleigh Mason, who's only being polite.

'Kate,' I reply. 'She's around somewhere. We saw you play at Glastonbury a couple of years ago.'

'You did? Shame the weather wasn't better,' she says. 'It was a fun day, though.'

'It was. You did a brilliant set.'

'Aw, that's kind of you to say. So what do you do, Ed?'

'Music teacher,' I reply. 'Actually, I think we studied at the same uni. You went to Manchester, right?'

She laughs. 'You went to Manchester, too? Small world! What do you play?'

'Piano, guitar mostly, clarinet.'

She perches on one of the couches, wobbling slightly but she catches herself. I think she's the only woman here in jeans. It's a nice change.

'Woo, too much Jack for me!' she says, giggling. 'You know what, Ed? We should play something together.'

'Seriously?'

'Sure, why not? Let's do it! Me and you ... you and me ... oh, and maybe my husband, if he's not too plastered already.'

'You're kidding,' I say, wondering if this is some sort of elaborate hoax. 'He's here? He's a tremendous bass player.'

She nods, looking around. 'Well, he better still be here; he has my cigarettes. Oh, there he is! DARREN! HONEY! FANCY A SONG? ED'S GOING TO JOIN US.'

Darren nods and waves over at me while the other guests start to applaud and cheer.

'Go, Eddie,' Lauren yells, while Graham sticks his thumb up. At least, I think it's his thumb.

'You see that piano?' Ashleigh asks, pointing to the

corner of the room. 'You play that. Tara has some guitars in her music room.'

She jumps up and runs out the door to retrieve the guitars while I'm left speechless and panicking. I down my drink and consider fleeing but it's too late. Tara is now ushering everyone through from various parts of the house and I'm trapped. I walk to the back of the room and say hi to Darren while his wife brings through two guitars. Behind her, I see Kate, standing beside Dolly, with her mouth open. I know how she feels.

'Well, you lovely people, it turns out that Ed and I both studied at the same university, and he plays piano, so I thought we'd have a song.'

Oh, just kill me now. I sit down at the piano and hope that either the lid won't open or that a second piano falls on top of me. It's one thing playing for fun and entirely another playing with professional musicians, no matter how tipsy they are.

'What shall we play, Ed?' Ashleigh asks as she fixes her guitar strap. 'What do you know?'

'Jingle Bells?'

She laughs. 'How about something for your girlfriend?'

I look at Kate. '"One More Day",' I reply, without hesitation. I must have played that on the piano a hundred times because it's one of Kate's favourite songs.

'You got it,' Ashleigh says before counting us in.

My nerves initially get the better of me, so we start over,

but I know this song like the back of my hand. As I play, I can picture Kate, sitting beside me at the piano – sometimes just listening to me sing and sometimes singing along in a key vastly different to the one I was playing, but it didn't matter. All that mattered was making her happy, just like it does right now.

As we finish, I look over at Kate and I see that she's applauding harder and louder than everyone else.

Darren leans in. 'Great job, dude. You killed it.'

'He sure did,' Ashleigh agrees, giving me a hug. 'You surprised the shit out of me, Ed!'

'I surprised myself,' I reply, laughing. 'Thanks for letting me play with you.'

'Which one's your girlfriend?' Ashleigh asks.

'Woman with the red hair, leather trousers,' I say. 'That's Kate. If you can say hi, I'd really appreciate it.'

'You got it,' she replies. 'I'll get us both a drink, though she looks like she might need a double.'

Kate

My hands still stinging from my rapturous applause, I try to process what I've just witnessed. Even as Ashleigh frickin' Mason walks towards me with a glass of Prosecco, I can't take my eyes off Ed. He was unbelievable.

'Your boyfriend plays beautifully,' she says, handing me the drink. 'If I didn't play myself, I'd hire him in a heartbeat.'

'You're Ashleigh Mason,' I tell her, like she doesn't already know. 'Why . . . how . . . I mean Ed never plays in public. I always said he should but—'

'My fault,' she replies. 'I tend to get up and sing when I've had a few. I'm afraid Ed just got dragged into it. He should play more, though, I agree.'

'This is so bizarre,' I say laughing. 'Sorry, I'm usually far more composed – and, well, sober.'

She laughs. 'Don't worry. I'm two drinks away from dancing on that nice coffee table. Oh, Ed says you guys saw me at Glastonbury last year?'

'We did. Though I first saw you about six years ago supporting Regina Spektor and I'm trying very hard to be cool here and not just tell you how much I love you.'

'Well, I think I love you more,' she replies, downing her wine. 'Oh, here he is! I was just telling your lovely girlfriend how amazing you are.'

Ed smiles. 'I'm still stunned that happened. My students will never believe me.'

'Oh, someone will have had their phone out,' Ashleigh says. 'Someone always bloody does. You can't take a wee these days without somebody filming it. Speaking of which, do excuse me.'

She darts off to find the bathroom, leaving Ed and me alone.

'Did all that actually happen?' I ask, almost fixed to the spot.

He smiles. 'I know. I am wondering whether someone's spiked the drinks and I'm just hallucinating.'

'She's tiny in real life, isn't she?'

Ed nods. 'I have year nines taller than her.'

'You were really great,' I tell him. 'It's been so long since I've heard you play that song.'

'Kate, do you think—'

'HOLY SHIT, THAT WAS DEADLY!' Graham thunders over to congratulate Ed, with Lauren following quickly behind. 'I've never heard you play like that, fella; I've only heard you tinkling the ol' school ivories.'

I watch Ed rub the back of his neck while he tries to absorb the compliment. 'Yeah, it was fun!'

'Well, this kicks the arse out of clubbing any day,' Lauren adds. 'Have you seen the master bedroom, it's huge?'

'I haven't, no,' I reply. 'But more importantly, does Tara know *you've* seen the master bedroom?'

She grins. 'I mean does anyone really *know* anything, it's—?'

'Do you mind if I steal Kate for a moment?' Ed interrupts, while I laugh at Lauren.

'Course you can, Eddie,' Lauren replies on my behalf. 'I'm going to get Grizzly Adams here a drink.'

'Somewhere a bit quieter maybe?' Graham suggests, as I watch him follow Lauren like a lost puppy. Did she just pinch his arse? God, I feel like I've been transported to an alternate universe.

We exit the living room and find a small cinema room off the hall. This house just gets better and better. I close the door behind me.

'Did you just see L and—'

'I know – nothing makes sense anymore. Look, I thought we should talk. I haven't handled everything as well as I could have and . . . well, I'm sorry. I shouldn't have put you on the spot back there, with Graham.'

'I don't even think he'll remember,' I reply. 'Look Ed, this has been hard on both of us.'

'I'm not sure how we got here,' he admits. 'It all seems so stupid now.'

I frown. 'I know exactly how we got here, and I said I didn't want this, Ed! You're the one who wanted to "see who you are without me". And from tonight, I can see that *without me*, you're someone who plays with established musicians at the drop of a hat, when I couldn't even get you to do karaoke down the pub!'

'Woah, hang on. You're the one who started all this, remember? Living a life that you don't want. How I have no ambition. What, now you're upset that I'm performing again? I thought that's what you wanted?'

'That's not what I'm saying.'

'Or are you upset that I did it on my own terms. Without you.'

'No! It's . . .' My voice trails off as I realise that's exactly what it is. Four days without me and he's already gone back to what he loves.

I sit down on one of the cinema seats. 'Did I hold you back?' I ask him. 'Clip your wings?'

He sits beside me and sighs. 'No, Kate, I did that all by myself. I've never met anyone so invested . . . so eager for me to live my best life. You just became frustrated that I didn't have the same determination. Tonight . . . that just happened by chance.'

We sit for a moment, listening to the noise of the party continue outside the room.

'I've missed you,' I tell him. 'Lauren sings Pink Floyd in the shower. You know I hate Pink Floyd.'

'I know,' he replies. 'And I've missed you, too, Kate but—'

'I know, I know,' I say. 'Nothing has changed. God, I'm sick of hearing that. I should go.'

He doesn't reply. Instead, he just bobs his head in acknowledgement. I pick up my bag and make my way to the door.

'Happy New Year, Kate,' I hear him say behind me.

'Happy New Year, Ed,' I reply, but I don't look back. I say my goodnights to Tara, get the house keys from Lauren and slip out the front door. By the time my Uber comes, I'm a mess.

JANUARY

Kate

'Well, it's a little different from the photos but it's definitely liveable,' Lauren says, looking around. 'I mean, it's only temporary, right?'

The photos online of this 4.2-star-rated, one-bedroom Airbnb looked stunning. Clean, bright, modern, lots of leafy, green plants and a beautiful view of the river. However, upon closer inspection, the plants are fake, the dust is real and every cupboard and drawer practically unusable, due to the amount of junk left either by the owner or previous guests.

'Why did I tell Ed to stay in the flat?' I ask her. 'I should have stayed there! Our lovely home with ample storage space, plenty of street parking and a comfortable couch that's not made of the same material used in a fucking slip-and-slide!'

'Maybe you should calm down a little,' she suggests. 'It's not as bad as—'

'It is! Every kitchen drawer and cupboard I've opened

is crammed full of someone else's clutter!' I storm over to the kitchen and pull open the drawer under the oven.

'A DVD player! Who the hell puts a DVD player in a kitchen drawer?'

'People who have Netflix?' she offers.

'I'll tell you who – the same person who stuffed these kitchen cupboards full of books and empty photo frames!'

As I fling one open, a frame falls out and on to my foot, making me yelp.

Lauren comes over and takes my arm. 'OK, let's just have a seat on the slip-and-slide and take a breather, shall we?'

I half laugh, half sob and accept defeat. I've only been in here for a few days, but it already feels way too long.

We take a seat as she tries to comfort me but I'm now bawling.

'I've even had to buy one of those portable clothes racks as the wardrobes are full of bed linen and jigsaws!' I cry, like a toddler. 'This is horrible.'

'But the bathroom is nice,' Lauren replies, reaching for any silver lining she can find. 'Lovely wet room and those body scrubs beside the sink are spa grade.'

'I know,' I reply, sniffing. 'My skin has never been softer.'

'See! You can do this. You've lived in much worse. Now let's open this wine, shall we?'

I nod and blow my nose while she goes to find a bottle opener. She may be some time.

Ed

'Sir . . . Sir!'

I look up from my computer screen and see one of my most annoying year 10s waving both hands in the air like he's trying to marshal a plane.

'Yes, Soroush?'

'I don't get it,' he informs me. 'This notation stuff. Like, they all look the same, just weird symbols.'

I look at my watch. Eight minutes until the class ends and he's telling me this now, instead of thirty minutes ago when he started. I signal for him to come to my desk, which he does, bringing his work with him.

'So you have to match the musical note to the length of the beat, yeah?'

He nods.

'And on this sheet here is a lovely chart, designed by me, showing the note, the name of the note, the length of the note and the corresponding rest symbol. You with me so far?'

More nodding.

'So you'd look at the note here, find it on the chart and then draw it on the stave. After all the notes are in place, you'll be playing and identifying the song.'

He's not nodding.

'Soroush?'

'What's a stave?'

I sigh, pointing to the lines on the page of the blank music sheet. 'Ringing any bells?'

'But how do we know what line to put it on?' he asks.

'Soroush, we ran through this in the last lesson. Each line and space has a note name attached. Remember the note G – always placed next to the swirly bit on the treble clef because it's also known as the . . .?'

'Triple clef?'

I want to bang my head repeatedly on the desk until he leaves. 'The G clef,' I reply, sighing. 'Where the swirly bit in the middle of the G clef meets the line, that's the note G. So what note comes after G?'

'H?'

'There is no H note in music, Soroush. There is however an H in homework, which I'd really recommend you do every now and again.'

He stares at me blankly, while Suzanne at the front of the class giggles. I don't know why she's laughing – *she* thought that *composition* was the stuff you put in the garden to help the plants grow.

'A, B, C, D, E, F, G,' I tell him. 'That's all the main musical notes. They just repeat, on and on and on. So A always follows G, just like D always follows C. It goes line, space, line, space. So if G is on this line, what note do we put in the space directly above it.'

'. . . A?'

Hallelujah, I think he's got it.

'And we can easily remember these by our acronyms. The lines, EGBDF – every good boy deserves—'

'Fellatio!' I hear a voice say from the back of the room. I really want to laugh but as a teacher, I can't be seen to be encouraging sex jokes in my class, no matter how amusing. 'Any more of that and you'll be staying an extra hour after school,' I tell Aaron Wiley, who tries to act all innocent but forgets he's the only boy in class whose voice hasn't dropped yet.

'Football,' I continue, 'and in the spaces, the word FACE from bottom to top, showing the position and letter of the notes. This is all on Google classroom. I suggest you take some time to go over it again.'

The bell finally rings, and I dismiss everyone, especially Soroush, with a wave of my hand, like a Roman emperor. As they leave, I hear Aaron say, 'He used to be able to take a joke. He's been a right moody git recently.'

The fact that I immediately want to add on an additional year to his detention for his cheek means he's probably right. I am a moody git, but it's hard not to be. This separation has been much tougher than I could ever have imagined. I thought being away from Kate at university was hard, but unlike uni, now I can't call her. I can't meet up with her on the weekend. Every part of me wants to text her and tell her Aaron's remark but that wouldn't be appropriate, no matter how much I miss making her laugh.

I hang back in class for a bit. I'm not in any rush to get home and I have access to a proper piano here instead of my Roland FP90 keyboard, which is sitting in a box under the bed gathering dust. Kate bought me that with her first proper lawyer wage and I've barely touched it. I suddenly feel decidedly ungrateful.

'Now you have no excuse not to do gigs!' she'd said. 'All those open-mic nights you've been procrastinating about, all those songs you've been working on . . .'

'All those people just waiting to tell me I suck,' I'd replied, facetiously. 'Can't wait.'

'God, have a bit of faith in yourself! Honestly, Ed, you're so bloody talented. Don't waste it. Besides, so what if someone thinks you suck? I think Liam Gallagher sucks, but I doubt he goes to sleep on a giant pile of money, worrying whether I like his music or not.'

I vaguely remember making some lame joke about 'rock and roll never sleeping', but when I think back to then, it makes me realise just how much she believed in me. Before university, I had all these ambitions to become an incredible singer–songwriter, but once I got there, I saw just how many people were in the same position as me, and all of them just that little bit more confident or talented or charismatic. By the time I graduated, I'd already applied for a fast-track teaching qualification. How could I expect Kate to continue believing in me, when I didn't believe in myself?

I close the classroom door and walk over to the piano, knowing that I'll have at least an hour before the cleaners arrive and the sound of an industrial Henry Hoover will drown me out.

My fingers start playing 'Please, Please, Please, Let Me Get What I Want' by The Smiths, but I soon start to smile as I hear Kate's voice calling me a drama queen, before going into a rant about Morrissey and his political views. I stop and take a deep breath. How am I supposed to play anything that isn't melancholy when that's what's seeping from practically every pore in my body? It's awful not knowing what she's doing . . . what she's feeling. She's probably having the time of her life in that Airbnb while I'm sat in a classroom, not wanting to go home to an empty flat and declining drinks with friends because I'm not ready to tell everyone that we've split up. I'm such an idiot. All she ever did was support me and encourage me and I chose the easy way out because I was too scared to even try. I could have talked to her, explained things. But instead, I just dismissed her and forced her to be brave enough for the both of us.

I take out my phone and Google open mic, London. About 51,800,000 results. I was not expecting this.

As I scroll through, I start to get a tad overwhelmed. Maybe I should start somewhere small? Local. You've just played with Ashleigh Mason, you pussy, I tell myself. You can certainly handle an open mic.

I search again for my local pub, The Tawny.

Open mic night every. Thursday at 8pm. Free drink for all performers. Come early and come prepared!

Feck it, I think. Even Liam Gallagher had to start somewhere.

Kate

'Whoever said that cooking for one was an enjoyable experience was lying. In fact, I'd go so far as to say it's stressful.'

Staying at this Airbnb has been an eye opener to say the least and there hasn't been a day when I haven't chastised myself for being so quick to leave our home. I put Gubba on speakerphone while I rummage around in the fridge.

'Kate, you cooked for yourself all through university, surely this isn't any different?'

Gubba is still the only one besides Lauren I've told about the break-up. I'm almost certain Ed hasn't told his parents as I haven't received a tearful phone call from Yvonne – and there would have been tears – which is why I also haven't broken the news to my parents either. I'll wait until my own sadness subsides before I take on theirs.

'Gubba, I lived on twelve-pence noodles and whichever ready meal cooked fastest in the microwave. I was too busy to learn how to cook and never home long enough to care.'

'In my day, we learned to cook at an early age,' she

informs me. 'I was cooking family dinners by the time I was thirteen. Your mother should have done the same.'

'Yes, yes,' I reply. 'Gen X bad parents, millennials have no life skills, I get it. If I'd anticipated that I'd be living in an Airbnb at twenty-nine, googling "things to do with eggs", I might have paid more attention to how my meals were prepared.'

I can hear the smirk on the other end of the phone. 'So what are you making?'

'Well, I wanted to attempt that Spanish omelette recipe you gave me, but I really don't understand it. You said cut thick slices of potato but not how to cut the onion. Is that thick, too? Cubed?'

'Just cut it until it's smaller than it once was, love. You'll be cooking it down, anyway.'

'OK, fine . . . and then you've said to partially cover the potatoes and onion and stew for fifteen minutes?'

'Yes.'

'What does that mean?'

She gives a little chuckle. 'Just chuck them in the pan and let them simmer for a bit.'

'You could have just said that,' I mumble. 'And then I just mix it with the egg, let it rest for fifteen mins and then fry it?'

'Exactly,' she replies. 'Though remember, while it's cooking, use your spatula to shape it into a cushion.'

'Into a what?'

'A cushion,' she repeats. 'Nice and padded around the edges. And just use a plate on top of the pan to flip it – much easier. Anyway, love, need to rush – the chiropodist is coming round at five. Let me know how you get on.'

She hangs up before I can ask her about cushions and plates. I can already tell this is going to be a disaster.

I should have just followed a YouTube video, but Gubba's omelettes are quite unique and I'm feeling a little homesick, if I'm honest. I also feel a tad embarrassed that I'm so useless on my own. Gubba's right. I should have paid attention to Mum cooking, but also to Ed. He made everything at home and not once did I think of asking him to teach me. It never occurred to him to offer to teach me either. I think we both just settled into our relationship roles, neither of us expecting that one day we might not be together.

Living here has opened my eyes to so many things. For someone as fiercely independent as I am, I've realised how little I actually do when I'm at home and how much I rely on Ed. It's the small things, like cleaning and replacing the coffee filter before bed so it's ready for me in the morning. Cooking every night because he gets home first, and he knows I'll be ravenous when I get in; or the fact that new toothpaste always appeared like magic after the old one had run out. While I'm not entirely incapable of fending for myself, it's been so long since I've had to do it. At university, Lauren and I halved in for a cleaner once a week, who admittedly was awful and ate all our yogurts, but saved us having to try and figure out how to clean the hoover filter. Even Lauren is more domesticated than I am, and she used to cook fish fingers in the toaster. God, I miss those days.

2011

Durham – Kate

'Hot water's off again,' I hear Lauren yell from the bathroom. 'Can you check the boiler?'

We knew when we moved in here that the rent was cheap for a reason, but after two years, I'm beginning to think we should be charging the landlord instead of the other way around.

Living above a supermarket in Durham city centre isn't as glamorous as it sounds. The landlord rents out this two-bedroom flat for £480 a month because it's tiny, old and the second bedroom is actually the living room, giving us no lounge area to sit in and bitch about him.

I close my laptop and walk into the hallway, throwing open the cupboard door. I sigh and scowl at the world's noisiest, most unreliable boiler. It's so old, I feel like I should be viewing it from behind an oil lantern.

I bang on it first, for no other reason than I hate it, before checking the pressure gauge. Unsurprisingly, it's at zero. I turn the knob and watch it slowly rise back up to 1.5.

Before I lived on my own, I had no idea what a boiler pressure gauge was, let alone how to maintain it. My handyman skills have dramatically increased in many areas, including radiator bleeding, plug changing and, most recently, wall-hole filling, after my attempt to hang a picture went horribly wrong. That's an area I still need to work on.

I turn the boiler on and off and wait to hear the pilot light kick back in, feeling very smug when it sparks into action. 'All done,' I yell back at Lauren. 'Might take a while for the water tank to heat up again, though.'

A few moments later, I hear the bathroom door being flung open, as Lauren stomps through to my bedroom.

'How the hell is anyone going to let me touch their hair, when mine looks like this?' she asks, pointing to a blonde frizzy mop which gives mine a run for its money. 'I knew I should have showered last night.'

'Well, you didn't get in until three am,' I remind her. 'And it would have been pretty rude to leave whoever the hell you brought home waiting.'

'You heard us, huh?' she asks, smirking. 'Sorry.'

'I think most of Durham did,' I reply. 'Though she was considerably louder than you. I think I prefer it when you bring men home. Their moaning decibel range is far easier to sleep through. I thought for a moment you were murdering Kate Bush.'

'Well, fear not,' Lauren says, sitting on my dressing-table

stool. 'I'm going to be at some Wella colouring course in London next week, so you'll have the entire place to yourself. Maybe Ed could come down? Produce a few decibels of your own?'

'Tempting,' I reply. 'But I've got so much on. Plus, Allison's on holiday next week and I said I'd take on some extra shifts.'

'I don't know how you do it,' Lauren says, opening and sniffing a tub of my moisturiser. 'Call Centre jobs are the worst. Crammed into a little cubicle and having to ask permission to go to the toilet. Customers either hanging up or being pissy with you . . . no thanks.'

'It's not too terrible,' I reply, watching her repeatedly stick her nose in and out of my Olay. 'I just zone out when they start complaining about their terrible broadband signals. Besides, the money isn't horrible, and I don't have to touch people's dandruffy heads, unlike some.'

She pauses and nods. 'True. Though a bit of dandruff isn't too much of a hassle. It's when they rock up with stinky hair that's not been washed for a week, or they've ignored a raging fungal scalp infection and expect you to deal with it.'

'And you think call centres are the worst?' I ask, feeling ill at the thought of a fungus-infested scalp. 'I'd have to disagree.'

'Overruled,' she replies, banging her hand on my dressing table. Lauren finds it hilarious to make lawyer jokes and is convinced that my life is going to be like an episode of *Suits* or *The Good Wife*. She forgets this is Britain, and also the real world. If the law students I've met are anything to go by, the chances of meeting some handsome, yet maverick and mysterious lawyer who will tear me away from Ed are less than zero.

'Anyway,' I say, waiting for her to stop laughing at her own joke, 'I need the cash for meeting up with Ed. Hotels and train fares aren't cheap.' I signal to her that her dressing gown is in danger of falling open.

'You've hardly seen him recently, though,' she replies, covering herself up. 'You both must be climbing the walls.'

'We're not animals!' I reply. 'We don't need to shag every five minutes. I'm no doctor, but I'm fairly certain nothing will close up or fall off if we don't have sex for a couple of weeks.'

'Well, I'm no farmer, but I can still smell bullshit,' she replies. 'You're nineteen not ninety! You're just as obsessed with sex as the rest of us. Are you bored with Ed?'

'What? No, of course not! L, can you stop sniffing everything on my dressing table – it's weird.'

'I mean, it would make sense. You've been together for a hundred years already. I get bored after a week.'

'I am not bored with Ed,' I insist. 'In fact, I'm speaking to him later. Now can we just drop this? I have revision to get on with.'

She puts down my hairspray and spins around on the stool. 'Fine! I have a lukewarm shower to get to, anyway.'

She flounces back out and I open my laptop. *Philosophy of Human Rights Law. Example of human rights are the right to freedom of* . . . I am not bored with Ed . . . *religion, the right to a fair* . . . I mean, it's been great being away from Castleton and experiencing new things, but that doesn't mean I'm bored with Ed . . . *trial, the right not to be tortured* . . . and maybe being alone has been good for me . . . *and the right to receive an education* . . . FINE, I'm not bored with Ed, but god, the pressure of trying to maintain a long-distance relationship when I have a million other things going on is exhausting. However, if Lauren thinks I'm bored with Ed, maybe he does, too. I take out my phone.

Hello! Lauren's away next week! Can you come up? xx

I need him to know that it's not him, it's me . . . but without having to say that overused phrase.

2011

Manchester – Ed

'Want anything from the shop, fella? I need to get more bog rolls.'

I look up from my phone to see Graham's head peeking around the lounge door. Graham's the only one here not studying music, instead opting for History and Sociology, and sometimes I think he feels a bit out of place. But he shouldn't. He's incredibly funny and likeable, if a tad odd at times.

'Are you wearing my hat?' I ask, narrowing my eyes at the grey beanie he has on. I already know the answer, as Graham does this all the time. If you leave anything lying around the shared lounge area, Graham will take it and either eat it or wear it. 'I was looking for that this morning.'

'Aye, I wondered who this belonged to,' he answers. 'It's pure cosy, innit? I'll just keep it on. It's Baltic outside, man.'

Considering I wear that particular grey beanie most

days, I think it's obvious who it belongs to, but he's too nice to argue with. Like me, the two women who live here, Ruth and Carly, also tend to put up with Graham's little idiosyncrasies, given that one of these is a strong desire to clean the kitchen every evening. I'll happily give up my hat to avoid doing dishes. Even the uni cleaners who come in once a week hope he never leaves.

'I'm good,' I tell him. 'But thanks for asking, mate.'

'No bother,' he says and disappears back into the hall. Three seconds later, I hear his cheerful Irish brogue asking Ruth if she needs anything. She yells back that he ate all her Pringles, so he'd *better fucking buy more*. He quickly agrees as Ruth is far scarier than the rest of us.

I open a can of Coke and go back to my phone, hoping she doesn't notice her cereal has also mysteriously reduced in quantity. At least I had the sense to eat it privately.

A few minutes later, Ruth appears, wearing her own hat and a bright orange padded coat which looks warm, if not a tad ridiculous. It looks like the bottom bit of a bouncy castle.

''Sup, Eddie,' she says, pulling her gloves out her pockets. 'Are you doing any open mics this week? I need someone on guitar.'

Ruth's studying music and drama. She's a really lovely girl, if somewhat pushy – but I guess you have to be to survive auditions. Our other flatmate, Carly, I already know from summer camp, so it's been great having a friendly face around. She spends most of her time with her boyfriend, though. He moved here with her, so he's obviously understood that long-distance relationships are bloody hard. Mum and Dad met Carly last time they came down and absolutely loved her, but then Mum does have a really soft spot for the Welsh accent.

'Nah, I need to work,' I tell Ruth, admiring her gloves. The palms have skeleton bones on them. 'I have a couple next week, I think.'

'Well, give me a shout if you change your mind, or get fired or whatever. I could really use you.'

The music scene in Manchester is every bit as vibrant as I'd hoped. It's also bursting at the seams with fellow singer–songwriters, like Ruth, who spend every waking moment planning their next gig. In Castleton, I was like a lanky enigma. No one else played as well or took music as seriously as I did. But here, I'm just another muso, trying to find his place in a city with a thousand others like me. Being here has been a blow to my ego. Any delusions of grandeur I had have been well and truly quashed. The more I gig, the more I realise that while I might be good, I'm not sure I have what it takes to be great.

I hear my phone buzz.

Hello! Lauren's away next week! Can you come up? xx

It's Kate. As happy as I am to hear from her, it feels like she's been dodging my calls lately. We used to talk at least twice a day and now I'm lucky to get five minutes with her between classes and her job. I try not to get upset with her, but I also do both, *and* tutor, and would still drop everything to grab a few minutes to say hi. I miss her. She makes me feel like I can accomplish anything, but when I have to deal with this shit alone, I'm hopeless. Sometimes I still feel like that kid in year 10, trying to make friends with the cool girl at the lunch table. I know that I need her more than she needs me and that's a disconcerting place to be.

JANUARY

Kate

Tara Mitchell has been keeping me busy with an endless stream of calls and emails. She even popped into the office this afternoon for an impromptu powwow.

'So I've been thinking about his request to do the fifty-fifty split with the kids,' she announced, while I scrambled to hide my lunch in my desk drawer. 'And while I know it's just an excuse not to pay child maintenance, I actually think it's a great idea.'

'You do?' I asked, choking down my chicken baguette. 'Well, that's encouraging. Custody can be one of the trickiest parts of a divorce to negotiate but I'm glad—'

'Because if he thinks for a second that walking coat hanger is going to want to play step-mummy, he's in for a rude awakening. I've seen her manicures; those claws aren't built for parenting. She can barely open her Birkin, never mind wiggle a straw into a Capri-Sun.'

'OK—'

'The moment they snot, poo or vomit on her, it'll be

game over. And they're three – it's unavoidable. So let him think he can play happy families. It'll be hysterical to watch. Besides, I could do with a couple of nights off – at least until he realises that my nails look like shit because I'm hands-on with the twins.'

I got the distinct feeling that words about nails had been exchanged between the pair of them, but I didn't dive any deeper into it. To me, her nails seem completely normal, but then I've never been one for acrylics. Maybe short, unpolished nails are grounds for divorce in their world.

'Right, well, if that's all, I'll give his solicitor a call later and we—'

'You're not married, are you?' she asks, her gaze darting towards my left hand, which I instinctively place on my lap in case she inspects my nails too closely and demands another lawyer.

'I mean, you brought Lauren to the party, instead of a partner which, I have to say was a godsend. My hair has never looked better.'

Lauren took on seven new clients from that one party, each with a huge Instagram following. As for me, despite leaving early, I did get a call from Jade Hart. We're just talking at the moment, but Harriet is delighted.

For a second, I was almost tempted to tell Tara that Ed was actually there, so she didn't think I was just a sad old spinster who drags her more impressive friends around with her.

'Well, no, I'm not married,' I replied. 'It's never been something—'

'Smart,' she responded, rising from her chair. 'Though why would you? You're dealing with unhappy, dysfunctional couples all day – that's enough to put anyone off marriage for life! Better run. I'll let you get back to your lunch.'

She left just as quickly as she arrived, but her words hung around much longer. Even now, I can't shake them. *Unhappy, dysfunctional couples*. This perfectly describes my parents. Their toxic relationship shaped the way I saw marriage, long before I ever started working here. I came into this job believing that marriage was a waste of time, and have surrounded myself with clients who only compound that belief. How on earth did I not think this would affect my relationship with Ed – a man whose views on marriage have been shaped by happy, functional parents and who's never doubted he'll have the same. Well, until I came along and screwed everything up, that is. I realise now that it was never marriage that I objected to. It was ending up like everyone else.

Ed

'So if you turn to page 78, you can—'

'Sir, was that really you on TikTok?'

I wondered when this was going to come up. Ashleigh was right. Two hours after our impromptu New Year's Eve sing-song, a rather shaky thirty-second video appeared online. Thankfully, as I have no social media, I wasn't tagged directly and managed to avoid being dragged into any online discussions. My students, however, aren't going to let this go quietly.

'It was, Lily,' I reply. 'Now if we can get back to—'

'But how do you know Ashleigh Mason?'

'I don't really, we just—'

'My mum said the papers said you were going to do Eurovision.'

I chuckle. Kate would love that idea; she's a huge Eurovision fan. 'No, that's not true. Funny, but no.'

'How come you never teach us stuff like that?' Lily asks.

I think this is the most she's ever spoken in my class. 'Like, you play proper well.'

'I mean, the curriculum dictates what I teach and—'

'Class might be more interesting if you did,' I hear a voice mutter. 'Instead of all this rubbish.'

I glance over at Scott Wilkins, one of the many smartarses I have in my class this year. I'm tempted to ignore his rude remark but as I seem to have everyone's attention, I decide to respond.

'This *rubbish*, Scott, is necessary not only for passing the class but to give you an insight into music. How it's constructed, delivered and, most importantly, how we can appreciate it on different levels. Of course, the academic side will never be quite as thrilling as picking up an instrument and playing, and yes, there are people who are self-taught – naturally gifted and can't read sheet music to save their lives. But for everyone else, it takes hard work and practice.'

Scott slumps back in his chair, still unconvinced that anything I have to say has any value whatsoever, despite my rising TikTok fame.

'Do you even like music, Scott?' I ask him. 'I mean, do you listen to it?'

'Course I do,' he replies. 'Who doesn't? But all this stuff is just boring. No one cares. It's all done on computers, anyway.'

'OK,' I reply. 'Who do you listen to? Favourite band? Singer?'

He shrugs.

'I mean you don't look like a typical Ariana Grande fan, but maybe that's your bag?'

'He listens to grime, sir,' Aaron informs me. 'Thinks he's going to be the next Stormzy.'

The class laughs while Scott tuts, dismissively. 'Like he's gonna know anything about—'

'British rap?' I ask. 'Lots of influences in there, like Jungle, techno, hip-hop. I personally prefer Wiley's earlier stuff, but Stormzy's killing it right now.'

Scott looks at me like I've just stepped off a spaceship.

'So Stormzy or Wiley or Dizzee or any of these artists – how would you describe their music?'

'Well, they talk about—'

'No, not their lyrics; we're not breaking down poetry here – just the music. How would you describe it?'

Scott shifts uncomfortably in his chair. 'Um . . . fast?'

'Exactly. It's usually around 140 beats per minute, giving it that driving bassline you kids love so much.'

Everyone sniggers, including Scott.

'And what kind of instruments are involved in grime music?'

'Drums,' he replies. 'And, like, computer sounds. Electronic.'

'Breakbeats, good,' I reply. 'Anything else?'

'Anything, man. You can sample any instrument.'

'Exactly. While grime is quite percussive with its use of drums, it's also extremely eclectic, but if you want to *make* grime music, you have to know the basics. In fact, the basics are the same for any genre of music, whether it's classical, country, pop, death metal or dubstep, whatever. If you want to sing, you need to know pitch and melody. If you want to rap, you need to know tempo, you need to know bars – how many words in a four-count beat. So this "rubbish" is actually the backbone of every song that's ever made you smile, dance, cry, feel inspired, and whether you choose to continue learning and go on to write, compose, produce, play or just stay at an appreciation level, it's anything but boring.'

The bell rings, putting an end to my little lecture. They all pile out of class, and I sigh, wondering whether I'm actually making a difference here at all. As I reach for my bag, I hear Scott clearing his throat behind me.

'Yes, Scott?'

'Sorry about earlier, Mr Morrison. Your class ain't boring, I . . . I just don't get it.'

I lift my bag and turn to face him. I'm surprised by how sincere he looks. 'OK. Well, I appreciate the apology.'

He nods and starts to leave.

'Scott. Wait a minute. If you were struggling, why didn't you come to me?'

He shrugs. God, teenagers are annoying.

'OK. I'm here every day after school. You let me know when you can stay late and we'll get some extra tuition in.'

'Any day,' he replies. 'I ain't got nothing waiting at home.'

In that moment, my heart breaks a little. Not only because of his answer, but because I feel exactly the same.

'Take a seat,' I tell him. 'No time like the present.'

Kate

When I was a kid, Gubba used to always say that I could sleep through an earthquake, admiring my ability to achieve coma-like status while she was lucky to get even five hours a night. Although my sleep schedule has been somewhat haphazard since joining Parish Scott Taylor, I still manage to sleep like the dead, every chance I get. That was until I moved here.

It's not only that the neighbours are unreasonably loud; it's that when I lie down at night and close my eyes, my mind instantly wanders to Ed. Wondering what he's doing, who he's seeing, what he's thinking. I have torturous, yet mildly hilarious visions of him and Carly playing their bloody clarinets together in bed, finally free to do weird shit without me getting in the way.

I've also taken to running over every stupid thing I've ever said and done. And there's a lot to choose from. As awful as it sounds, I'm hoping that his life is just as empty as mine right now because the thought of him being fine without me is too painful to bear. I've been so careless with him and now he's probably having the time of his life at home, without me, and undoubtedly sleeping like a baby. So tonight, I'm sleeping over at Lauren's. I'm hoping that a friendly face might ease my mind, or at least provide me with enough booze to knock me out. It's been a while since we properly hung out and I'm really looking forward to it. It'll also be the first time I've been in her new flat since she moved in last month.

It doesn't take me long to pack a bag, considering I haven't really unpacked properly since I got here. I just lift some pyjamas and clean underwear from my case and throw them into a backpack and grab a bottle of wine from the fridge – one of the only places in this flat that's used the way it's intended.

When I arrive at Lauren's flat, I double-check the address she's given me. I'm in Battersea, but this absolutely isn't the 'quiet little block of flats' she described to me. I drive under an arch and into the residents' parking, finding her two designated parking spots. I recognise her bright yellow Honda electric car and pull up in the spot beside it.

This 'quiet little block of flats' is a private, purpose-built residential development right on the riverside. It looks like a holiday complex, with a sandstone court area, displaying lots of real, dust-free plants in oversized pots. I find her doorway and she buzzes me in.

'Jesus Christ, L,' I say, as I enter her flat. I look around, open-mouthed, like I've just stepped into the Warbucks mansion. 'What do your clients pay you in? Gold? The way you described it, I thought you'd moved up near Clapham Junction.'

'Oh, shush,' she replies. 'I got a good price; the owner needed a quick sale. I think he was on the run or something. I didn't ask in case he thinks I know too much.'

Lauren always plays down just how well she's doing, financially. Like somehow, it's crass to admit it. Or maybe she just didn't want to shove this massive flat in my face while I'm currently living out of a suitcase.

'Want the tour?' she asks.

'Yes, I bloody do,' I reply, throwing my bag down. 'Lead the way.'

'God, this place has everything,' I remark, as she shows me around. Her main bedroom is twice the size of mine. 'You even have heated floors! What sorcery is this?'

We go down a small set of stairs which leads to the huge open-plan living room and kitchen.

'You have an island?' I say. 'We don't even have room for a table in our kitchen. You're making me incredibly jealous here.'

Lauren opens a bottle of wine with a corkscrew shaped like a pirate. She bought that when we shared a flat at uni. 'Don't be daft,' she tells me. 'All it takes is one bad dye job from me and I'm back to living above the Tesco Express again.'

'Hey, I liked that flat,' I tell her, as she hands me a glass of red. 'There was a certain charm to only being able to fit one person in the kitchen at any given time.'

She grins. 'That microwave in my bedroom was an absolute lifesaver. Reeked, though. Never heat up a curry in a room the size of a postage stamp.'

I laugh. 'When Ed and I moved into our house, we only had a microwave for about six months. I caught him trying to make toast in it once. Idiot.'

'Well, I'm glad you brought him up first,' she says, gesturing at me to follow her to the living room. 'I mean, I'd ask how you're coping but, well, you're here and you're not sleeping.'

'How did you know that?'

She plonks herself down on a huge grey couch. 'Your eyes brought their own bags with them.'

'All right, fine. Maybe I'm not sleeping too well but it's to be expected, right?' I reply, sitting beside her. Sweet lord, the sofa is comfy. 'It'd be weird if I wasn't missing him. I mean, even after I murdered you for this flat, I'd still think of you fondly.'

'Glad you still have your sense of humour,' she says, sipping her wine. 'It'll come in handy when you're writing your Tinder profile.'

'If you're going to make fun of me all night, you'd better have snacks.'

Three glasses of red and a sharing bag of Kettle crisps later, I finally admit to Lauren how much I miss Ed.

'You know, I thought throwing myself into work would help,' I tell her. 'But that's literally all I've been doing for the past three years, anyway. So nothing has changed – except that I have no one to sound off to when I get home.'

'Yeah, I get that,' she replies. 'But – and no offence – that must have made you a barrel of laughs to live with . . .'

She's right. I never realised just how much I unloaded on to Ed and how patient he must have been to sit there and listen, especially to the inane drivel I came out with night after night.

'I've blown it,' I tell her. 'He'll be sprawled out on my side of the bed, unburdened, probably speaking sexy German to Carly while she plays her goddamn clarinet in the buff. I can see it now. *"Oh, ja, Carly, das ist gut. Ich komme!"'*

'Google translate?'

I nod. We spent five years in the same French class. I know as much (or as little) German as she does.

She giggles. 'I very much doubt that. And I doubt that you've blown it either. You're just going through a rough patch. He adores the shit out of you. That'll never change.'

'I'm not so sure,' I reply. 'I told him I didn't want to split up anymore, remember? He's the one who decided it's what we needed.'

'So maybe you need some big, grand gesture,' she suggests. 'Like when Kevin Costner took a bullet for Whitney Houston in *The Bodyguard*.'

I pour the last of the wine, laughing. 'OK, A – that was his job; and B – no one is trying to shoot Ed. Not that I know of, anyway.'

'Well, you should do something,' she replies. 'You can't just live in an Airbnb and translate basic German forever.'

'I know, I know,' I concede. 'I'll figure something out.'

'Ooh!' she exclaims, making me jump. 'What's that annoying eighties' film you both love?'

'There's more than one,' I say, wiping the red wine off my chin.

'That one you both made me watch, and I hated it.'

This pretty much applies to every film we watched together as teenagers. Lauren tends to favour movies made after she was born, preferably starring Whitney Houston.

'Do you remember who was in it?'

'Nah. I just remember a scene where the guy had a big nose, and she was like, *You have a massive nose and I love you* or something.'

'*Roxanne*,' I inform her. 'How can you hate that film? It's hilarious. Steve Martin is—'

'Fuck, it's like drinking wine with Mark Kermode. Listen, you should do that.'

I frown. 'Tell Ed he has a big nose? I mean, granted it's not small but—'

'No, tell him you love him for who he is. That you love him regardless. Unconditionally. Just like she loved big-nose guy.'

'Charlie,' I inform her. 'His name was Charlie.'

'I don't care.'

'And I do love him unconditionally!' I insist. 'I really do.'

'Even with that hair?'

'What's wrong with his hair?'

'Nothing,' she replies. 'Just wondering.'

'Talking of hair, how did your date with Graham go?'

Since New Year, Lauren and Graham have been texting profusely.

'Good,' she replies. 'Well, incredible, actually. I don't think I've ever met anyone as funny and sweet in my life.'

I cough.

'Sorry, any *man*,' she clarifies. 'But he's just so different from the guys I normally date. They're usually all Yeah! Football! Cars! Manly shit! And he's like university-educated and has no sense of style and god, that beard is annoying but—'

'You really like him, huh?'

She beams. 'I really do.'

'Then I'm happy for you,' I reply. 'He's one of the good ones.'

She nods. 'And so is Ed . . .'

*

Although the company (and the wine) was great tonight, I still can't sleep. It doesn't matter where I am, I still miss Ed. I miss hearing him breathe beside me or moaning that my feet are too cold before doing his best to warm them up. Lauren's right. I do need to tell Ed I love him. Because if I were him, I'd be in doubt. I need to tell him that it's not him I'm frustrated with, it's me. It's always been me.

When I graduated from law school, I was passionate about justice. About giving a voice to those who felt silenced. I wanted people to know that I was in their corner, that they could rely on me to fight on their behalf. I wanted to come home at night and feel that I'd made a difference, no matter how small. I thought that I *could* make a difference at Parish Scott Taylor, but I was wrong. And not only wrong, but too proud and stubborn to face it. Maybe it's time that I did.

Ed

'I know I've been busy lately, but you should have let me know that you and Kate had actually split for good. Jesus, I thought it was just a wee lovers' tiff! You didn't seem that bad at New Year.'

Graham hands the barman a twenty-pound note as I take a sip from my first pint of the evening. 'Why?' I ask. 'It's not like you could have done anything.'

'I could have held you.'

I smirk.

'Look, maybe I couldn't have done anything, he continues. 'At least I can turn my break-up into a quick ten-minute set for shits and giggles. But you still need someone to talk to. I can't believe Kate moved out. Lauren didn't say a word. Where's she staying?'

'Airbnb in Shoreditch,' I reply. 'Might as well be Mars. Lauren, eh? You two getting cosy these days?'

'We're courting,' he replies. 'Taking things slow. I want

to make sure she's the one before I let her near my beard, you know?'

'Not really.'

He takes his change from the barman and throws it in the tip jar. 'I am sorry, though. You must be gutted.'

I prop up the bar, continuing to sip my pint, while Graham waits for his Guinness to settle. 'I've been all right,' I tell him, not wanting to admit that I've been miserable as sin. 'Not much venting needed, to be honest. It's just one of those things.'

Somewhere under Graham's very unkempt brown beard, he frowns. 'But the fact that you're down here doing an open-mic night tells me otherwise. I've been there, remember? Everyone thought I was having some sort of mid-life crisis at twenty-five.'

'You were, though,' I remind him. 'You literally quit your job and bought a bearded dragon.'

'You leave Penelope out of this.'

I laugh. 'This isn't the same. I'm not looking to change career; I'm just trying something new. Shaking things up a little – it's no big deal.'

'Most men join the gym after a break-up,' Graham remarks, his pint froth nestling on his top lip. 'Get guns and abs! They don't throw themselves to the wolves.'

'You did.'

He shrugs. 'I already had abs.'

We both laugh. Graham's a lot of things, but buff isn't one of them.

I turn and look towards the back of the room, where a solitary mic stands on a small stage. The Tawny hosts one of London's best open-mic nights, where anything goes: comedy, music, magicians. It's usually mobbed, and tonight is no different. The room is already filling up with punters, ready to be entertained for free and getting cockier with each drink. I'm nervous as hell. I haven't performed my own stuff in public since I was at university, and apart from the impromptu song with Ashleigh, I haven't performed publicly in years. Well, apart from playing piano for the school drama productions but that doesn't count because no one was there to see me.

'This is scarier than I anticipated,' I admit.

'Aye, it's never easy,' Graham replies. 'But you're a teacher. A classroom full of hormonal teenagers is far scarier than anything these idiots could throw at you.'

This is true. My first year of teaching, an entire class refused to quiet down for me, until I yelled so loudly my voice cracked. They then spent the rest of the period giggling and impersonating me. I was devastated. Children are brutal.

An attractive woman in leather trousers comes up to Graham and asks for a selfie. He politely obliges while I look on in amusement. This is the guy the kids at school used to call Beardy Brannigan, a man who packed the same lunch every day for three years and who was twenty before he realised that a scarecrow was so named because it scares crows. And now he's a frickin' celebrity!

'Don't,' he says, catching me grinning as she walks away. 'I hate all this shite. It's embarrassing. Twitter is going to be filled with photos of me drinkin' the black stuff and smiling away like a proper wee Irish twit.'

'You should be honoured,' I tell him. 'Women like that only approach me to ask me to move out of the way. How did they even get you to do a set here? You're a big-time TV star now.'

He snorts. 'One TV show does not a TV star make. Besides, I asked *them* if I could perform. I started out here. It's rough but it's great fun. I come back here every now and again to try new material.'

'How rough?' I ask, my palms beginning to sweat a little. 'I mean, has anyone actually died from doing this – because I feel like I'm about to have a heart attack.'

'Put it this way: if they hate you within the first three seconds, you'll know about it. Um, does Kate know you're doing this? Is she likely to come?'

'Nah,' I reply. 'I mean, she always pushed me to do stuff like this but . . .'

'You don't want her to think you're doing it just cos she told you to?'

'No,' I reply. 'Nothing like that. I just don't want her turning up and seeing me fail spectacularly.'

'Understood,' he says. 'She already has enough reasons not to be with you, right?' He grins, unable to keep a straight face.

'Exactly,' I reply, laughing. 'I'm reluctant to add "dies on his arse on stage" to her list.'

He nods and takes a swig of his Guinness. 'Do you miss her yet? I think it took me about a month to actually miss Sheena. Up until then it was all revenge thoughts and walking around wearing her shoes so I'd stretch them out.'

'I do miss her. Every minute of the day,' I reply, my heart pausing from its impending failure just long enough to plummet down into my stomach. 'The house is empty without her, and I don't just mean literally. It's like . . . everything is a bit meaningless without her there. What's the point in cooking from scratch for one? What's the point remembering funny shit that happened at work with no one to tell when I get home?'

'What's to remember? You teach at Braidstone High. Nothing funny ever happens there.'

'Fair point,' I concede. 'But you know what I'm saying. It's about sharing the little things.'

'See – you did need to vent,' Graham mutters under his breath while I prattle on.

'And I miss just being near her,' I continue. 'Her smell, her hair, the way she—'

'So the sex, then?' Graham says. 'I get that. The rest of

the stuff you get used to but the regular, no-stress, early-morning shagging? *That* I miss. The whole one-night stand thing is far too much pressure after a while, but I take it you're not at that stage in your recovery.'

'Mate, I'm not even interested in my hand, never mind anything else.'

'Ooft,' he replies, grinning. 'Hopefully, a bit of that pent-up frustration will serve you well tonight. Just please don't depress everyone with ten minutes' worth of sad love songs.'

I squirm. Now he tells me. 'I mean, they're not *all* sad.'

'*Five minutes, everyone.*'

'You ready?' he asks. 'Ready to just go at this, head first, pedal to the metal, balls to the wall?'

I down the dregs of my pint and take a deep breath. 'Nope,' I reply. 'But here goes nothing.'

FEBRUARY

FEBRUARY

Kate

I've been staying at work as late as I can, just so I don't have to come back to the Airbnb, sit alone and dwell on things. God, I do love a good dwell, unlike Ed who's probably moved on already. He'll definitely move on before I do. I'll be hearing about his lavish wedding and birth of his first child before I've even considered signing up to a dating app. I used to hate his go-with-the-flow, carefree attitude and now I'm wishing I had even a tenth of his disposition. Maybe then I wouldn't feel so goddamn wretched.

'Coffee?'

The sound of our receptionist Trish's voice snaps me back to reality.

'I'd love one,' I say. 'Just black. Thanks so much.'

'Black?' she questions, her eyebrows rising high above her glasses. 'What happened to one sweetener and a dash of oat milk?'

I gesture to the pile of paperwork on my desk. 'I need

a direct hit tonight. These are going to keep me here for hours.'

She disappears back around the door and off towards the small kitchen at the end of the hall. It's not Trish's job to make coffee for anyone other than visitors but we've got into the habit of making it for each other. A tiny woman in her fifties, she barely reaches five foot, wears her black hair in a tidy, no-nonsense bun and speaks three languages. I like her very much, which is more than I can say about the majority of the staff here. I'm not entirely sure whether it's just my current state of mind but I'm finding my role here less and less fulfilling, not that I found it particularly rewarding to begin with.

'One coffee, black,' Trish says, handing me my mug. 'And some leftover biscotti from the four pm meeting.'

'You're too good to me,' I say, gratefully taking the plate.

She smiles. 'You work too hard. Get that nice boyfriend of yours to take you away for a weekend. Relax a little. Get some sun.'

'We both know that I burst into flames in direct sunshine, Trish,' I reply, deflecting the subject away from boyfriends. But yes, I should look into a weekend break. Good idea.'

She nods and leaves my office as I take a bite of my biscotti. I'd love a holiday. The last holiday Ed and I took was a cheap week in Tenerife, not long after Tom was born. We stayed in two-star self-catering luxury and ate tapas and fried bananas by the sea. After being apart at university for so long, that week really brought us back together on more than just a physical level. That was also the week my period returned with a vengeance and any fears of pregnancy were put to rest.

As I look at the files on my desk, I realise I don't have one case where anyone actually needs my help. There are no victims. No injustice. No hardship. I would kill for a client who actually had a reason to divorce other than infidelity or boredom. There are people in the world who need someone to fight their corner and I'm not going to find any of them working here. My phone rings before I have the chance to ponder this any longer.

'Kate, I have your dad for you.'

'Oh. Great, thanks Trish . . . Hi, Dad, how are you?'

'Good, love. How are you?'

'Oh, busy as usual,' I reply, my mind racing as to why he's calling. 'What's up?'

'I just wanted to let you know that the sofa came this morning. Cracking-looking thing. It's a beauty.'

'Brilliant,' I reply. 'I'd forgotten it was coming, you'll need to send me a photo.'

'I will,' he says. 'I'll get Sandra to take one on her phone, the camera's better.'

'Sandra?'

'Yes, the cleaner you hired. Sandra.'

I laugh. 'Of course. Sorry, for a second, I thought you

had some new woman stashed away. She's working out well, then?'

'Very well,' he replies. 'Beautiful woman. A godsend, really.'

'Dad . . .'

He doesn't reply.

'Dad . . .'

'Well . . .'

'Oh, Dad, you're not shagging the bloody cleaner, are you?'

'She's amazing, Katie! You'll really like her.'

'Of course I will. I hired her!'

'Don't be like that.'

'Like what? You're the one who said your therapist thought it would be inadvisable to enter into any new relationships while you're focusing on your sobriety.'

'Yeah, about that . . . I didn't think she was quite the right fit for me, so I'm not seeing her anymore.'

'Dad, are you drinking again?'

'No. I promise.'

I sigh, unsure whether I believe him or not. 'So you're involved with the cleaner and you've fired your therapist?'

'Yes.'

'But the couch is good?'

'Oh, yes.'

'Great. OK, Dad, nice to hear from you. I'd better get back. Speak soon.'

I stuff the rest of the biscotti into my mouth and crunch loudly. Deciding to help my dad get back on his feet has been more stressful than I anticipated. It's absolutely his right to find a therapist he feels comfortable with and to start seeing someone new, regardless of whether she's there to clean or not. I just have to trust him. And that's the problem. I'm not ready to.

Ed

'You should do one of those singing competitions,' Graham says, getting started on his third pint. 'You know like *X-Factor* or Britain's Got Idiots or whatever it's called. You've got that sad puppy-dog face those kinds of shows want. They could film you in school pretending you really like teaching, while also having a broken heart which only fame can heal.'

'Jesus, no thanks,' I reply. 'I can think of nothing worse than being famous. Shift over, will ya?'

I've just done my weekly ten minutes at The Sneaky Fox, a pub with the nicest craft beers and punters who won't try to bottle you with them. It's the kind of place I'd like to have brought Kate to. Fuck, why didn't I take her out more?

'So why are you putting yourself through all this if you don't want it to go anywhere?' Graham asks, looking genuinely bewildered. 'I don't get it.'

'Fun,' I reply. 'Coming out, performing, having a couple of drinks. It's fun! Like karaoke, but with my own songs.'

'So you're telling me that if someone offered you a record deal, you'd say no?'

'I would,' I reply. 'I mean if someone wanted to buy my songs – that I could definitely get behind.'

'Ah!' Graham exclaims. 'Smart move. Songwriting royalties are the way to go. All it takes is one shit, catchy Christmas song and you'll be set for life.'

'True. But it's not even just that. I've realised that as much as I enjoy this, I'm far happier during the creative process than I am in the performance side. It's a bit like teaching. I put the time and effort in and then I get to watch those kids flourish.'

'I'm going to need you to never say that again,' Graham says, frowning behind his beard. 'I think all that guitar strumming has gone to your head. You'll be pulling out your tambourine next and shaving your head.'

An hour later, I'm jumping in an Uber and heading home, having declined Graham's invitation to carry on drinking at his flat on a school night. Although it seems more favourable than going home to an empty house, I don't fancy listening to how great Lauren is while I'm busy missing Kate.

Kate

It appears this morning that an entire flock of birds has shit-bombed my car, which looks like a Jackson Pollock painting. I'm already running late but there's no way I can leave it like this. I get inside, fling my bag in the back and google the nearest car wash which, it seems, is a hand-wash service at the bottom of a car park. This is what I miss about living outside of London. Almost every petrol station at home has a drive-thru car wash where machines do all the work, and you don't feel uncomfortable having other human beings wash bird poo off your car.

Thankfully, I don't have to queue for too long and four men soon surround my car with soapy water and sponges, while I sit there like a princess trying not to make eye contact. Ed does this all the time and it doesn't bother him, but I just feel like I should be apologising for not keeping my car cleaner, like I have any control over avian bowels.

I get into work around 8am. I'm the last to arrive and it doesn't go unnoticed. Even the trainee receptionist, sitting beside Trish, gives me a look which can only be described as 'nice of you to join us'. I scowl back, hoping she messes up the partners' lunch order.

As usual, I barely slept last night but that was mainly down to my neighbours who decided to have a party which started at 12am and was still going when I left for work. I need to look for somewhere new. Maybe somewhere with underground parking.

By 10am, I feel a bit more on top of things, though Harriet has decided to assign me to a new case, with a meeting already scheduled for this morning. My phone hasn't stopped ringing which doesn't help. Between all this and the bird shit, I can tell today is going to suck.

'Kate, I have your mum for you.'

'Can you tell her I'll call her later, Trish, I'm just about to go into a meeting.'

Today has been a nightmare already and it's only half-past ten. I hang up but the phone immediately rings again.

'Sorry, Kate. She says it's important.'

Trish connects her while I carry on adjusting my notes for my meeting. I have no idea why Harriet wants me involved – this guy doesn't even have a regional accent or a social media presence.

'Hey, Mum, everything OK? I'm really up to my eyes in it. I've got—'

'Gubba's in hospital, love,' she says quietly. 'She's got a lung infection and it's bad.'

My stomach drops. 'When was she taken in?'

'This morning, about eight. Her breathing was pretty laboured, so the home help called an ambulance. We're here now.'

My mum is very rarely rattled by anything, but her voice sounds shaky . . . almost desperate.

'I'll come,' I say. 'I'll be there as soon as I can.'

'Thanks, Kate. I'll get Gary to text you the info.'

The moment she hangs up, I feel the panic begin to set in. Not Gubba. She has to be all right.

I grab my bag and rush to Harriet's office, almost breaking my neck as I go over on my ankle, snapping one of my high heels. I take my shoes off and keep going.

I knock on her door and enter barefoot. 'Harriet, sorry but I—'

'Something wrong with your shoes?' she asks, gawking at me like it's the first time she's ever seen feet. 'Maybe ask Trish or the new girl—'

'My gubb . . . grandmother is in hospital,' I say, cutting her off. 'I'm going to have to leave right away. Family emergency.'

'Sorry to hear that, Kate, but I'm afraid it's not a great time. We have that meeting. Do you have those notes for me?'

'What? Um, yes, they're on my desk but I don't think you understand. She's very ill and—'

'Let's just get the Humphries meeting over with and then we can re-evaluate. Make sure you find some shoes.'

Harriet returns to her paperwork, making it clear that the conversation is over. I leave the office stunned, shoe-less and even more panicked than I was before.

I get back to my desk and call down to reception.

'Hey, it's Kate. I was just wondering if you had any spare . . .'

I pause. *What the fuck are you doing, Kate? This job over Gubba? Really?*

'Hello? Are you still there?' I hear the trainee ask.

'Yes, sorry, if you could collect the Humphries files on my desk and give them to Harriet. My grandma is really ill and I need to be with my family.'

'Of course,' she says. 'Whatever you need.'

I manage a thank you before I hang up. I feel like I can't breathe. I grab my coat and move as fast as my bare feet will allow.

Ed

'Right, everyone, class dismissed. But please drop your worksheets in my basket before you go. Oh, and please don't do anything on the way home which'll be caught on someone's Ring doorbell – *Gavin.*'

Gavin smirks while the rest of the class rib him. A local resident emailed an impressively high-definition MPEG of Gavin, in his school uniform, rearranging some garden gnomes in what can only be described as a dwarfish orgy.

I'm packing up when my phone starts to vibrate in my pocket. It's Kate. My heart starts racing. I haven't spoken to her since New Year. *Oh shit, be cool, Ed. Be natural. Don't make her sorry she called.*

'Kate,' I say in my best casual voice. 'Hi. How are you?'

What follows is an incoherent rambling which is very hard to decipher. All I can make out is Gubba, work and shoes, amid crying and the occasional swear word.

'Slow down,' I say, switching my phone to the other ear as I turn off the classroom lights. 'I can't understand you.'

I hear her take a breath and sniff loudly into the phone. 'Gubba's in hospital, Ed.'

'Oh no! What happened? Is she OK?'

'Lung infection. It's all my fault. I gave her those cigarettes. Oh god, I've killed Gubba!'

'She didn't just start smoking,' I say, trying to reason with her. 'You gave her what was probably two out of hundreds, Kate. This isn't on you. What does the doctor say?'

'I don't know. I'm going to drive up there now. Mum's with her.'

'You're not driving anywhere, Kate,' I tell her. 'Not that distance, in this state. I'll take you.'

'You'd do that?' she asks, her voice one tremble away from a full-blown wail.

'Of course, whatever you need.'

'I need shoes,' she sniffs. 'I broke my shoes.'

We arrange to meet at Kate's Airbnb in Shoreditch, so she can dump her car and grab some shoes. It doesn't look like much from the outside – an old block of flats that needs updating – but there's resident parking, which I guess was part of the appeal. It's in a livelier area than our home in Croydon, but I imagine the rates here aren't cheap. I pull up beside her car and text her to let her know I'm here.

I hug her the moment I see her.

'Thanks for doing this,' she says. 'I'm all over the place right now.'

'She'll be OK,' I assure her. 'Gubba's a tough old bird and you know she's holding out for that telegram from the Queen.'

At least I make her smile. Shoes and clothes collected, Kate gives me the hospital address and we set off for the Peaks. I keep the conversation light. As much as I want to tell Kate how much I've missed her, I know now is not the time.

'I've given my boss a call and explained the situation,' I tell her. 'I'll keep her updated, but she'll arrange a supply teacher for tomorrow.'

Kate gives a little laugh to herself. 'You picked the right job, Ed. It must be nice to work for actual human beings.'

'What do you mean?'

'It doesn't matter,' she replies. 'Right now, none of it matters.'

It's almost 8pm when we get to the hospital, heading straight to ward 7. As we go up in the lift, a thought occurs to me.

'Kate, have you told your family that we've split?'

She shakes her head. 'Not yet. And now's probably not the best time to tell them either.'

'No, I didn't mean . . . I was just checking.'

The doors open and we follow the signs until we reach the nurses' station.

'Marian Adams,' Kate says to the nurse behind the desk. 'She was brought in today.'

'Room 2,' he tells her. 'Best make it quick – visiting hours have just finished.'

We cross to the other side of the ward and find room 2, where we can see Paula sitting at Gubba's bedside. Kate grabs my hand as we walk in.

'Oh Kate, love, you made it,' Paula says, quietly. 'She's sleeping; they gave her something for her pain. Looks like pneumonia.'

Gubba looks almost as pale as the sheets she lies under, with an oxygen mask over her mouth. I hear Kate gasp a little.

'What are they giving her?' she asks, pulling a chair up beside her mum.

'Antibiotics, oxygen,' Paula replies. 'They've done chest X-rays and god knows what else. Doctor says we'll know more in the morning. See how she's responding.'

'You look tired as well, Mum,' Kate says. 'You should get some rest; we'll take you home.'

Paula nods. 'They don't let visitors stay overnight, so I'll come back first thing.' She leans in to kiss Gubba. 'N'night, Mum. I'll see you in the morning.'

As we walk back to the car park, Paula suddenly stops. 'What if she's not all right, Kate? I can't lose my mum. I'm not ready.'

As she cries, Kate just holds her in the middle of the

corridor. I carry on to the car park to give them some time alone, wiping away my own tears. I'm very fond of Gubba – and while I might not be family, I'm not ready to lose her either.

Kate

When we arrive home, Tom's still up, and meets us at the front door with Gary in tow. 'Is Gubba OK?' he asks me. 'Mum says she's not well.'

I don't think I've ever seen him look so concerned before, and instantly, I know it's my job to make things less scary for him. I smile, hoping that my mascara-stained eyes don't give me away.

'Well, she was asleep when I saw her, but she had this amazing mask on. So I asked the doctor about it, and he said, "We're giving her super oxygen. This oxygen is so high-tech and advanced that everyone who takes it immediately gets stronger."'

'Really?' he asks, his face marginally less fraught.

'Yup,' Ed replies. 'They even X-rayed her whole body, and do you know what they found? I couldn't believe it.'

Tom's on the edge of his seat here. 'What?'

'I'll tell you,' Ed says, obviously trying to come up with

something quickly. 'He showed us the X-ray and we saw . . . biscuits! Hundreds of them.'

Tom starts to giggle. 'I don't believe you.'

'You don't believe me? You know when Gubba visits and then you're like "Where did the Jaffa Cakes go?" She eats them all. Honestly, I'm sure I saw a Wagon Wheel in there, too. She must have swallowed it whole.'

Now Gary is laughing. I glance at Mum, who's smiling but too exhausted to join in. I'm just glad we can make Tom forget what's going on. At least for a second.

'Now, I do believe it's bedtime,' Ed says. 'And if someone doesn't read me a story, I'll never get to sleep.'

Tom throws his hand up like he's in class. 'I have a book. We can read it together.'

Ed takes Tom upstairs while I ask if there's anything I can do. 'Dishes? Make tea? Anything?'

'Just being here is enough,' Mum says. 'You all right to sleep in Tom's old room again?'

'Of course,' I reply. 'I can get him ready and take him to school in the morning. Just go and get some sleep. Both of you.'

I make some tea while I clean up a little in the kitchen. It doesn't really need it, Gary's obviously been busy, but I need to feel helpful. I need to feel something other than useless. To add insult to injury, when I changed into my black ballet pumps, I failed to notice that the stitching was coming away from the right one. It's now hanging off and flapping as I walk. Thankfully I also grabbed my trainers, I'll just need to wear them tomorrow.

I'm halfway through my second cup when Ed creeps into the living room, his hair dishevelled.

'He finally went to sleep,' he tells me, gently closing the door. 'I had to lie with him for a bit.'

'There's tea in the pot,' I say, reaching for a cup. 'Come and sit.'

He nods and flops down on the sofa beside me and for a while we just sit in silence, both of us just processing the day.

'Bet you didn't think this was how your day would go,' I say, trying to be somewhat upbeat. 'Hope you didn't have to cancel plans.'

'Just an open-mic night,' he says. 'Nothing I can't do any other night of the week, it's no problem.'

'You're performing, Ed? That's amazing!'

As happy as I am for him, I'm also disappointed that he's not spent the past few weeks curled up in a ball crying. He's moving on.

'It's been . . . interesting,' he replies with a smirk. 'But the response has been mostly good.'

'Mostly?'

He grimaces. 'First time I went to a place near Covent Garden with Graham. I got through one song before someone yelled to get the bedwetter off stage. I've switched up my set since then. You can laugh, it's fine.'

I can't help but chuckle a little. 'How is Graham? Still doing that set about his ex? She'll be raging now he's on the telly.'

I met Graham's ex-wife, Sheena, once at the pub, but I wasn't a fan. I don't remember her laughing, or even smiling, the entire evening.

'He's great, actually,' Ed replies. 'Though he thinks we're a couple of idiots for . . .

His voice trails away. Perhaps this conversation isn't what either of us needs right now.

'Anyway, I can sleep on the couch,' Ed suggests. 'I'll tell your mum I wanted to let you rest. I don't think now's the time to get them up to speed with what's been going on.'

'I don't want to sleep alone,' I tell him. 'I'm sorry if that's selfish but—'

'It's fine,' he replies. 'You don't need to explain. We can do that.'

He stands and holds out his hand and leads me upstairs. In silence, we get undressed and, for the first time in weeks, Ed and I share a bed and he holds me until I fall asleep.

I've been up since half seven, making breakfast for everyone and a packed lunch for Tom, who guides me, step by step, on the correct way to make it. He pads around the kitchen in his pyjamas, watching my every move.

'Mum always cuts the cheese into blocks, not slices.'

'Does she? OK.'

'And she gives me milk, not juice.'

'No problem.'

'She cuts my sandwiches into triangles, not squares.'

'Triangles? Right-angled or Acute?'

'Cute.'

'Good choice. Now, can you go and put on Disney Plus because we don't have it at home and I'm really in the mood for something with an annoyingly catchy song I can sing to Ed when he wakes up.'

Tom hops off to the living room, while I simmer some porridge and attack an especially crusty loaf with a bread knife. I haven't cut a loaf in years; in fact, I'm not even sure we own a bread knife. At least I can make porridge from scratch, though I doubt that's going to earn me a place on *MasterChef* anytime soon.

I lay the table, popping some honey and jam into little ramekins, and fill up a jug with fresh orange juice. Yvonne would be proud. The truth is, I'm kind of enjoying myself.

Mum was told to call the ward after 9am, to see how Gubba fared overnight, so I let her and Gary sleep on. For now, I'm doing what I do best – staying focused. However, this feels different, almost unfamiliar. For once, my focus isn't fixated on my career or my clients. There is no long-term objective, no goal I'm striving for.

At quarter to eight, Gary appears, apologising for

sleeping in, while I hear Mum walk across the landing to the bathroom.

'Sit down,' I tell Gary. 'I'll stick the kettle on. Porridge is in the pot on the table, toast will be two minutes. Tom, sweetheart, come and eat. You need to tell me how terrible my porridge is, compared to Mum's!'

Gary sits at the table, not quite knowing what to do with himself, while Tom reluctantly leaves the television to eat.

Back in the kitchen I make a pot of tea and butter the toast, bringing it through just as Mum traipses downstairs.

'Get any sleep?' I ask. She shakes her head. 'Not really, love. I'm too worried.'

'Come and eat something,' I say. 'Tom's already at the table. Ed will be up once he smells the porridge.'

'Porridge?' Mum questions. 'You hate porridge. Did Ed teach you how to make it?'

'Gubba taught me,' I say, smiling, as I follow her through to the living room. Gubba was old school with breakfast when I was a kid. When I stayed over, she'd make porridge every morning, just like her mother used to, and sometimes Spam on toast, which I point blank refused to entertain. The porridge, I forced down with milk and honey, but it's never been a favourite of mine. Of course, Gubba then followed her porridge and Spam with a pot of tea and three fags, which she convinced herself was fine as she wasn't smoking on an empty stomach.

'I stole a pair of your knickers from the tumble dryer

this morning,' I tell Mum. 'I forgot mine. Packing under-wear wasn't exactly top of my list yesterday.'

'Oh, do they fit you?' she asks, pouring some tea.

Even in times of crisis, she'll still find a way to mention my weight. I just nod and bite my tongue.

After breakfast, I continue helping Tom get ready, making him laugh while we sing along to 'You're Wel-come' from *Moana*, a film he's watched at least three hundred times in his short life.

'Is Ed taking me to school, too?' he asks, rudely inter-rupting my word-perfect rap.

'Of course,' I reply on Ed's behalf. 'Though you'd better wake him up – he's still asleep. I think jumping on him ought to do it.'

Tom rushes upstairs, excitedly informing Ed he's taking him to school. I hear a loud 'Oof!' from Ed as Tom dive-bombs him.

'I used the last of the bread, so I'll pop into the shop after we take Tom to school.' I sit back at the table and pour some more tea. 'Oh, I'll pick up some flowers for Gubba, too. For her house. Make it nice for her coming home.'

'But what if she—'

I take Mum's hand and stop her before she can finish that sentence. 'She'll be home before you know it. I'm sure of it.'

Mum leans over and hugs me. 'You're such a kind girl,'

she says. 'I'm sure she'll love that. I wouldn't get lilies, though. She lets that weird stray cat in, and it might eat them, god knows, it eats everything else.'

Ten minutes later, Tom drags an unkempt Ed into the room, his face still faintly creased from the pillow.

'Turns out I have the important job of taking Tom to school,' he tells us. 'If I'd known, I'd have packed my best suit and tie for the occasion.'

He takes a slice of toast but doesn't sit. 'Come to think of it, I didn't pack anything. I haven't been home. Sorry, Tom, I'm going to have to accompany you dressed like an actual teacher. How embarrassing.'

'We're leaving in fifteen,' I tell them both. 'Have you done your teeth?'

'Not yet,' Ed replies, through a mouthful of toast. 'I didn't pack a toothbrush.'

'Not you,' I laugh, before telling Tom to run up the stairs and brush for two minutes, knowing he'll spend thirteen seconds, like every other eight-year-old.

Once we're all ready, Ed and Tom head out the door first while I hang back and speak to Mum. I can tell she's anxious. It's eight-thirty and she'll be calling the hospital while I'm out.

'Do you want to wait until I get back?' I ask, pulling on my coat. 'Or I can call for you?'

'No, I'm fine,' she replies. 'Gary's here in case . . . well, you know.'

'She's not going anywhere,' I reassure her. 'Not yet. I'll be as quick as I can.'

I open the bag with my trainers in and wince. *Oh, come on . . . you've got to be kidding me.*

I get about twenty feet from the house before I want to turn back. In my rush yesterday, I grabbed two pairs of leggings (one with a hole in the thigh), a thin red jumper that's seen better days and a white work blouse that doesn't fit properly across the chest. Not only that, but I also lifted the wrong shoe bag. Instead of my black Converse, I brought my bright yellow and pink hi-vis trainers, which I bought with the intention of doing a night-time fitness boot camp before remembering how much I hate organised exercise. I only have my green full-length Monsoon dress coat to cover this particularly ridiculous ensemble. Ed might be wearing the same clothes as yesterday, but at least he looks like a normal bloke with normal-coloured shoes. I look like I've been dressed by Tim bloody Burton.

I catch up to Ed and Tom, lingering behind for just a moment to appreciate how sweet Tom looks, swinging his little lunchbox while his backpack bounces with every step he takes.

'Hey,' I say, trying to slip in unnoticed but Ed doesn't miss a trick. His eyes immediately lock on to my fluorescent feet.

'Oh my . . . don't you just love Kate's trainers?' Ed

remarks, drawing Tom's attention to them. 'Aren't they just the brightest shoes in the whole world?'

I'm aware that Ed hates these trainers. He says they're the ugliest shoes ever designed. And that's coming from a man who once wanted a pair of Yeezys.

'Jessica Marlow has the same ones,' Tom replies. 'My teacher says you can probably see her feet from the top of Mam Tor.'

Oh, great now I'm wearing the same trainers as an eight-year-old. That's not humiliating at all. I see Ed smirk. 'Mam Tor's only five hundred and seventeen metres,' he remarks. 'I'm almost certain you could see those things from space.'

'Yes, fine, I packed the wrong trainers,' I confess. 'But at least I'm not wearing the same underwear.'

'Hey, I turned them inside out,' he replies. 'It was either that or borrowing a pair of Gary's old-man pants!'

Tom laughs and puts his hand in mine as we cross the street. It's so small, it almost catches me by surprise. I clasp it tightly as we dash across, getting more than one look of disapproval from nearby parents. Obviously, I should be setting a better example, but the only car in sight was a Fiat Panda, going about 5mph.

As we arrive at the gates, a gentle wave of nostalgia laps against my brain. This used to be my primary school, long before they fixed the roof and built the extension on the back to accommodate more kids from nearby villages.

I remember the large weather board outside reception, where every day one child would be chosen to place the appropriate symbols on the map of the town. There were piles of suns, clouds, lightning bolts, rainclouds, snowflakes and, my favourite, the wind faces, which had little puffed-out cheeks. I remember the hopscotch board painted yellow on the playground, the smell of school dinners, the little garden we'd all keep tidy and the vast amount of artwork displayed inside every classroom and on every corridor wall. Most of all, I remember being happy here. This is where I first met Lauren, hiding behind her mum, and wearing the most amazing pair of Lelli Kelly shoes I'd ever seen.

As soon as Tom sees his friends, he immediately drops my hand. I don't take offence; I was eight once, too. Being eight means you're almost nine and far too grown up for hand holding, even when you might still want to.

'Is Mum picking me up?' he asks.

'I'm not sure,' I reply, glancing at Ed, knowing that it'll depend on how Gubba is doing. 'Though, if she can't, I will. I promise.'

'Can we get ice cream?'

'In February?' I ask, grinning. 'It'll stick to your tongue and then you'll have to walk around like that until spring. How about a hot chocolate instead?'

'Deal!'

I steal a kiss goodbye and wave as he runs off towards

a small group of boys, but instead of stopping, he runs straight past, making a beeline for a tiny blonde girl with glasses and a unicorn lunchbox.

'That must be Paige, then,' Ed says with a little chuckle. 'Haha. Good lad.'

'It's kind of adorable,' I reply. 'I like her glasses. I wonder if we'd have been friends in primary school?'

'Doubtful,' he replies. 'Not with those shoes.'

As the school bell rings, the kids all disappear inside, except for one or two latecomers bolting down the pavement at high speed.

'I said I'd pick up some bread and flowers,' I tell Ed. 'Do you mind?'

'Not at all,' he replies. 'I might grab a coffee. I still haven't quite woken up yet. Wonder if the bakery still serves that rocket fuel they try to pass off as caffeine.'

Fifteen minutes later, we're armed with two crusty loaves, two potent coffees and a bouquet of purple freesias and white roses. We walk back towards the house, passing by the churchyard. But unlike at Christmas, our conversation is cordial. There's no anger, no blame, and any sadness we're feeling today isn't caused by the other.

'Thanks for last night,' I say. 'You've been so, so brilliant. I feel terrible for saying this, what with Gubba being ill, but I've almost enjoyed it.'

'Enjoyed what?'

'Making breakfast, taking Tom to school, buying coffee, being with you,' I reply. 'It almost feels, well, normal.'

'It's not terrible,' he says, as he keeps pace with me. 'It's understandable. It's not been the most pleasant time recently. A bit of normal is welcome.'

As we reach the house, I stop at the gate, taking a moment to gather my thoughts. 'Think Mum has called already? It's after nine.'

'Most likely,' Ed replies. 'She's not the type.'

'Yeah,' I agree. 'She's probably on the phone as we speak. You know, if Gubba's really not well, I'll have to stay down here for a bit. Help out.'

'I know,' he answers. 'I can go home and bring you whatever you need or even get some time off and be here with you, if that will help?'

His face looks so earnest, so kind. I can't help but place my hand on his cheek.

'Ed, you have a job to get back to. After everything, please don't feel obligated—'

'Kate, I'm here for as long as you need me.'

'Ed, I . . .' I try to reply but the words catch the back of my throat. There's so much I need to say to him, so much I regret, but at this moment, I can't find the words. So instead, I just take his hand in mine as we walk through the front door.

Ed

I can hear Paula talking in the living room as we step inside. I pause, trying to gauge her tone, but it's hard to tell with the living-room door shut. She's not crying, which I'm taking as a positive sign, but maybe we've already missed that part. Kate and I carry the bread, flowers, and empty coffee cups to the kitchen before joining her mum and Gary.

Kate isn't as hesitant as me, almost bursting through the door like the FBI.

'Did you speak to the doctor?' she asks. 'Is Gubba all right? Wait . . . why have you got your coat on? What did the doctor say?'

'Calm down, love. She's going to be OK,' Paula informs us. 'They're keeping her in for a day or two, but her doctor says she's much brighter this morning. It is pneumonia, but it's treatable and she's already responding well.'

'Oh, thank god,' Kate exclaims, bringing her mum in for a hug. 'Fuck, I was so worried.'

'Me too,' Paula replies. 'Me too. But she's a fighter.'

'That's brilliant news,' I say. 'You must be so relieved.' I sit on the edge of the couch, feeling slightly redundant. Gary isn't a particularly tactile individual, so hugging him would be beyond awkward, and I don't want to just throw myself on to Kate and her mum, like it's some kind of grief scrum.

It's touching, though, watching Kate and her mum together. I can almost see their worry evaporate as they comfort each other. Despite their disagreements, it's obvious they love each other; but I don't think there's a woman more loved than Marian Adams, and I hope that Gubba knows this.

'We're popping over to her place to get her some bits and pieces,' Gary tells me, his practical mode never switched to off. 'Apparently, she's been asking for her glasses and her phone.'

'She'll be wanting to play Wordle,' Paula remarks, picking up her handbag. 'She hasn't missed a day yet.'

'Me neither,' Kate replies. 'I do it first thing every morning with my coffee. Maybe I'll pick her up some crossword puzzle books later.'

I didn't know Kate was a Wordle fan – but considering she's usually out the door before I get up, how could I?

'Give Gubba my love,' Kate tells them. 'I'll come and see her tomorrow. I'm sure she could use some peace and quiet today, without me blubbering over her.'

'We'll be back in time to pick Tom up,' Gary says. 'Will you both be here for dinner?'

'I'll pick him up,' Kate insists. 'I was going to take him for hot chocolate.'

'And I'm going to stop by and see my parents,' I reply. 'So I'll probably eat with them.'

'Very good,' Gary responds before wiping his glasses on his jumper. 'You ready then, Paula, love? I've put the spare travel case in the car already.'

Five minutes later, Kate and I are alone on the couch. Her face looks visibly less anxious, the small lines between her eyebrows gradually smoothing out. She stares into space, just decompressing.

'Say hi to your mum and dad for me,' she finally says. 'Tell them I'm sorry I couldn't come round.'

'Yeah, course I will,' I reply. 'They'll understand, it's fine.'

'Have you told them about us?' she asks. 'You know, splitting up.'

I sit back on the couch and sigh. 'Honestly? I don't know how to. I've been waiting until . . . well, until I get my head around it a bit more. I still need to sort out where I'm going to live and if I'll even stay in London.'

'You'd leave London?'

'Maybe,' I reply. 'Fresh start and all that. I can teach anywhere.'

Kate goes quiet again. I get the feeling the conversation is over.

'I'll see you later tonight,' I say, standing up. 'Get some rest.'

I automatically lean in and kiss the top of her head before pulling back. 'Ah shit, sorry,' I say. 'Old habits.'

She pulls me back in and hugs me tightly before heading upstairs.

Kate

When my alarm wakes me at 2pm, it takes me a second to remember where I am, before it hits me. My first thought is relief that Gubba's going to be all right, closely followed by disappointment that Ed's not lying beside me like he was last night. My third thought is filthy and entirely inappropriate, so I spring out of bed, pretending it didn't happen.

Tom's school gets out at 2.45pm, which gives me time to grab a quick coffee before I have to leave. I feel like I'm running off coffee fumes these days, but needs must.

I borrow a pair of Mum's jogging trousers and head down to collect Tom. I decide to give Lauren a call, to update her about Gubba.

'Ha! That woman will outlive us all,' Lauren says. 'That's brilliant news.'

'I know,' I reply, hearing my trainers squeak as I walk. Have they always done that? 'I'm so relieved. Can you ask that person to turn off the hairdryer while I speak, it's very rude.'

'Sorry, your majesty, I'll go to the back,' she replies. 'Oh . . . is Ed still there?'

'Yup. He says he'll stay as long as I need him. He's been so great.'

'Well, that's because he is great,' she informs me. 'And fit. Great and fit. Men don't usually come with both of those qualities, you know. Or if they do, it's because they're like three foot tall or perhaps lacking in other areas.'

'I know . . . I know . . .'

'Listen, my client's just come in, I'll call you later. So glad about Granny. Love you!'

I tell her I love her too, but she's already hung up. I knew she'd drop Ed into the conversation. She's right, though. He is fit.

Tom runs out of the playground approximately thirty seconds after the bell, like something is chasing him. Nothing is, of course, he just likes to run. I've never fully understood that.

'Where's Ed?' he asks, looking around. 'I drew him a picture!'

'Nice to see you, too,' I say. 'Ed's gone to see his mum and dad, but he'll be back later. You still want to get some hot chocolate?'

'Yes!' he exclaims. 'Can I get marshmallows?'

'Hmm, maybe for a look at your drawing?'

'Deal!'

The fact that I have to basically bribe my little brother to interact with me is slightly troubling but at least it's working.

Blue Peak Café is busy, but we find somewhere to sit near the door. I haven't been here in about ten years, but it hasn't changed much. It still has the same exposed brick walls, the same blue-coloured tables and the best hot chocolate within twenty miles.

'Mum and Gary saw Gubba this morning,' I tell him as he parks his bag and lunchbox under his chair and sits down. 'She's coming home soon.'

His face lights up. 'Really? Did the oxygen work?'

'It did,' I reply. 'She'll still have a bit of a cold for a while but she's already much better.'

'Adam Grant's granny died,' he tells me. 'He said that he saw her in her coffin, and she was all rotten and she looked like this . . .'

He pulls a scary face and I can't help but laugh. 'Well, I think Adam Grant's full of sh . . . erm, nonsense,' I say, catching myself before he tells on me for swearing.

'No, he said her tongue was hanging out and her eyes were all bloody and gross.'

'Is this the same Adam Grant who told everyone his dad was The Rock?'

Tom nods.

'The same Adam Grant who said that he had a driving licence?'

'Yep.'

'And is his dad The Rock?'

Tom shakes his head. 'No, his dad works in that super-market Mum goes to.'

'Correct. And does he have a driving licence, even though you can't get one until you're seventeen?'

'He said it was a special one for kids.'

'So I think we can both agree that if he's making this stuff up, he's probably making up the stuff about his granny, right?'

'Right,' Tom agrees. 'Paige said that he was lying, too.'

'Well then Paige sounds like a very smart girl.'

'What can I get you both?'

'Oh,' I say, startled by the server. 'Can we have two hot chocolates please? Both with marshmallows.'

'Just what you need on this cold day, isn't it?' she says to Tom. He nods in agreement. 'Coming right up!'

Sometimes it's worth coming back to Castleton just to absorb the friendliness that exudes from the people here. I mean, not everyone, of course – but compared to London, it's practically a different planet.

'Here,' Tom says, slapping down a piece of paper in front of me. It's his drawing. I turn it over and begin to study it.

'This must be Ed,' I say, pointing to the tallest figure in the middle. 'You've even got his stubbly beard right. Well done. And this must be you – because I'd recognise that lunchbox and cool hairdo anywhere.'

Tom beams. He's obviously put a lot of work into this.

I look at the last figure and start to laugh. 'And this must be me,' I say, trying to catch my breath. 'Tom it's so brilliant!'

'That was us walking to school this morning,' he tells me. 'It was really fun.'

The figure on the end is all dressed in black, with scribbled red hair and bright yellow feet, like two large bananas. My trainers. Ed's going to die when he sees this.

But then I notice something, and my laughter subsides. Only I'm holding hands with Tom in the drawing. Just me. I don't know what it means to Tom, but to me it means everything, and my heart melts. I throw my arms around him.

'I think this is the best drawing I've seen in my entire life,' I tell him. 'And I've seen the *Mona Lisa* in Paris.'

'Adam Grant said the *Mona Lisa* isn't real.'

'Adam Grant's a moron,' I reply. 'But you, my darling brother, are quite the artist and I'm even going to buy a special frame for this. Ed's going to love it, too.'

Tom hugs me back and giggles. 'Love you, Kate.'

I swallow the lump in my throat and tell Tom that I love him, too.

Ed

When I pull up outside Mum and Dad's house, their car isn't there. A bright red Peugeot SUV with this year's plates has taken their space and I just know that when they get back, Mum is going to throw a fit. She's as protective of her parking space as she is of me.

I walk around to the back of the house where I hope that they haven't moved the spare key from under the broken slab at the bottom of the garden. They've been hiding it here since we moved in. Thankfully, it's there, right next to a giant spider which remains still while I have a small freak-out. God, I hate them. Kate is far braver when it comes to insects. She even gives tired bees sugar water in the autumn.

I open the front door and am as surprised to see Dad as he is me.

'Ed! We didn't know you were coming, son. Why didn't you ring the bell?'

'I thought you were out,' I reply, closing the door behind me. 'Your car isn't there.'

'We got a new one!' Mum yells from the living room. 'Did you see it? What a beauty she is.'

I take off my coat and follow behind Dad, a smell of fresh bread wafting from the kitchen. Mum's on the couch, feet on the pouffe, dipping bread into a bowl.

'That Peugeot is yours?' I ask, peering into her bowl. 'What was wrong with your Honda?'

'Failed its MOT,' Dad answers. 'Would have cost more to fix than the car's worth.'

'Cracking car,' I say. 'I didn't think you'd get anything so modern.'

'Neither did I,' he admits. 'But we decided to spoil ourselves. Besides, it's far easier to get in and out of with my back. And it has heated seats.'

'It's ever so comfortable,' Mum adds. 'The man at the dealership even showed me how to connect my phone so we can answer calls while we drive.'

'Living the dream,' I say, smiling. 'Good for you.'

'You want some tomato soup?' Mum asks. 'I can open another tin.'

'Nah,' I reply. 'I just want a dunk of yours.' I take some bread and dip it in the soup, being careful not to drip it on myself or the carpet. I sit down beside Mum.

'Kate not with you?' she asks. 'Is her granny any better?'

'Pneumonia,' I tell her, going in for a second dunk.

'She'll be all right, though. Hopefully out of hospital soon. Kate's hanging back to help out with Tom. She sends her love.'

'Well, that is good news,' Dad says. 'Pneumonia's bad at any age but in the elderly, it's vicious.'

I love how Dad refers to the elderly like he's not in that age bracket. Although maybe seventy is the new fifty these days, I have no idea.

'Do you mind if I have a nap?' I ask. 'I got quite a broken night's sleep last night.'

'Your bed's there,' Mum says. 'Will you stay for dinner? We were going to get some Chinese.'

'That sounds lovely,' I reply. I feel bad for thinking it, but it's nice to be here instead of at Kate's. No stress, everyone is well and I can just be myself for a little while.

I go downstairs and kick off my shoes, collapsing back on the bed. I'm exhausted. Kate fell asleep in my arms last night and I didn't have the heart to move her. Actually, I didn't want to move her. I've missed her so much. However, that meant I only nodded on and off the entire night. Also, she snores like a beast.

Dad knocks on the door at six and tells me that the food is here. I didn't realise I had slept for so long. I'm tempted just to stay in bed, but I'm starving, so I give my face a quick wash and head upstairs, following the smell of fried rice and MSG. As usual, Mum's laid out the dining table, even though I'd be happy with a plate on my knee in front of the telly. I love the way she puts out chopsticks, even though we're all too ham-fisted to use them properly.

'I just ordered you mushroom curry,' Mum says, 'and some veggie wonton.'

'Perfect,' I reply, pulling out a chair. 'Kate will be sorry she missed this. She loves wonton.'

'Well, take her some back,' Dad suggests.

That's not a bad idea. Maybe she could use a little wonton after the day she's had. 'Yeah, I think I will,' I reply. 'Thanks, Dad.'

Dad tells me all about the features on his new car, most of which I can guarantee he won't use. Still, it's nice to see him excited about something and I'm really happy that they finally got rid of that nineties' Honda Civic that must have had about ten million miles on the clock.

'And what's new with you, son?' he asks, passing me the rice. 'School going well?'

'It's fine,' I reply. 'Same old. I have been doing some open-mic nights, though.'

'Performing?' Mum asks. 'How wonderful!'

I nod. 'I was a bit rusty, but it's been fun.'

'Then you must play something for us,' she exclaims. 'That old piano hasn't been used for a while.'

'Sure,' I reply. 'Maybe after dinner.'

As mortifying as that sounds, I don't have the heart to say no. Music is such a huge part of Mum's life, the least I can do is let her watch her boy perform. We finish dinner and go through to the living room.

'When was the last time this was tuned?' I ask Mum. 'Must be a while.'

'Last month,' she replies as I pull out the stool. 'It's just a habit now, I suppose, even though I don't play often.'

As I lift the lid, I feel four years old again. Me, sitting staring at the black and white keys, too short to reach the pedals, while my mum sits beside me, showing me where to place my fingers. I should have played more when I came home to visit but the desire to play for fun was long gone. Well, until recently.

I start to play, and I start to sing and before long, my mum is crying, and my dad isn't far off. It's a song about love. It's a song about mistakes. It's a song about Kate. I always knew I'd write a song about her; I just didn't expect it to be this one.

Kate

We arrive at Gubba's sheltered-housing complex in Bamford, armed with some shopping, her flowers and a couple of puzzle books to help her pass the time. Ed parks up near the front and we carefully make our way along the path, being careful not to slip on the ice. It's colder in February than it was at Christmas, but still no sign of snow.

'You'd think they would grit these paths,' Ed says. 'Someone will do themselves a mischief.'

'I'm glad I wore my trainers,' I say, carefully dodging the especially shiny parts of the path. 'They've got good grips.'

'I think I'd rather break my leg than wear—'

'Ugh, I get it. You hate them,' I say, making a mental note to complain to the council . . . or the warden . . . or whoever is responsible for elderly wellbeing around here. I knock gently on the door and wait, wondering if Mum remembered to call and tell Gubba we were coming. There's no answer so I knock again. I have the spare key, but I really don't want to just barge in in case Gubba's walking around with no knickers on. It's happened before.

By the third knock, I'm beginning to worry and decide that seeing my grandmother's bare arse is the price I'm willing to pay to ensure she's OK.

'Wait here for a second,' I tell Ed, turning the key in the lock.

It's 11am but the living-room curtains are still drawn which is very unlike Gubba. She's one of those people who wakes up at half-five in the morning and considers this a perfectly reasonable time to get up. The living room and kitchen are open plan, which means Gubba has less of a distance to travel but also no kitchen table to sit at. I know she misses that. Her kitchen at home was the hub of the house. The place where she'd share meals with my grandpa, where my mother would finish homework after school, where I'd sit and colour in while she made her famous pressure-cooked potatoes with butter and chives. Now she's resigned to eating in a recliner chair in front of the television.

I place the flowers and the shopping in the kitchen before tiptoeing through to the bedroom. I crack the door open, just enough to see she's in bed. Her room here is much smaller than the one in her old house. I used to love her old bedroom. It was the brightest room in the house, with dark oak furniture and a recliner beside the window that she'd sit and read in during the summer. It's nice enough here, but everything reminds me that she's no longer as capable as she once was. And my god, she was capable.

'Gubba?' I say softly. 'Are you awake?'

No response. I move a little closer.

'Gubba?'

Again, no response. No movement. I watch the bed-covers. Is she even breathing?

My heart races as I make my way to the far side of the bed. She looks so peaceful. So still. Oh, Gubba. My hand slowly reaches down to touch her face. It feels . . .

'JESUS BLOODY NORA! GET OUT OF MY HOUSE!'

I scream and jump backwards as Gubba shoots upright in bed and throws a teacup at me.

'Gubba, it's me!' I yell, as the matching saucer whizzes past me. 'Stop throwing stuff!'

'Kate?' Ed rushes in, almost knocking the door off its hinges. 'You OK?' he asks, his eyes darting between me and Gubba, who's now scrambling for her glasses.

'In the name of God, Kate,' she says. 'You scared the life out of me! What are you doing, slinking around here in the middle of the night like creeping Jesus?'

'Middle of the night? It's eleven in the morning!' I exclaim. 'And I called your name. Twice! I thought you'd bloody died on me.'

'Eleven?' she questions. 'My goodness. Those tablets the doctor gave me must have knocked me out. Hello, Ed, dear.'

'*You* nearly knocked *me* out with that cup,' I mutter, my heart rate slowly returning to normal. 'Thank god your aim sucks.'

Ed starts to snigger.

'I forgot Paula said you'd be round,' Gubba says, throwing back her covers. 'Did you bring me my tea? The home help brought that supermarket stuff that tastes like dishwater.'

I hear Ed give a little 'yikes' as he quickly spins around and makes his way into the hall. I dash to help Gubba pull down her nightdress. She might be wearing underwear, but she still seems a little out of it.

'I brought bread, tea, milk and some other bits and pieces,' I tell her. 'We just wanted to visit before we drive back to London. See how you are.'

'That's nice, love. Go and put the kettle on, while I have a wee.'

'Do you want your dressing gown?'

'Thanks, love.'

I return to the kitchen where Ed's making himself useful, putting the shopping away and opening the window to let some fresh air in. At least it doesn't smell of smoke – that I'm grateful for.

'Text your mum to bring more salt,' Ed says, holding a container of table salt. 'I'm going to chuck this on the path.'

He vanishes outside and I put the kettle on before popping some bread in the toaster. I can at least make sure she eats something before I go. I feel like all I've done lately is worry. About Gubba, about Mum, about Tom, about Ed and me . . . Christ – I was even worried that Luther, the dog from the café, might have got sick from eating that muffin. As hard as it's been, Gubba being ill has put things into perspective. All the needless concern I have over the future, over my career, doesn't seem so important anymore. If I've learned anything over the past few days, it's that everything can change in the blink of an eye.

Gubba strolls in and takes her seat in the living room, all wrapped up in her dark blue dressing gown and matching slippers.

'I'll just bring your tea,' I tell her, grabbing the toast as it shoots up. 'What do you want on your toast?'

'Nutella,' she replies. 'There should be a jar in the cupboard above the toaster.'

Gubba's sweet tooth is legendary but sometimes she really does have the taste buds of a ten-year-old. Just like me.

I set everything down on the little table beside her chair, then bring through the milk and sugar.

Ed reappears, with an empty salt container. 'I've done your path, Gubba. Last thing we need is anyone slipping.'

'Oh, and Mum's coming over at one,' I tell her. 'She's collecting your prescription as well.'

'I wish you'd all stop fussing,' she insists. 'I'm hardly on me last legs. It was just a chest infection.'

'It was pneumonia,' I remind her. 'And you scared us all. So fussing is not optional, I'm afraid.'

She smiles. 'You can be just like your mum sometimes. Though she makes a better brew.'

I roll my eyes. 'And you sound just like Tom . . . but at least the colour's back in your cheeks. You were so pale earlier.'

'Probably because you scared the rouge right off my face!' she replies. 'Any more toast?'

'I'll get it,' Ed offers, taking her plate. 'Same again?'

'Please.'

She watches Ed walk to the kitchen and smiles. 'It's been a long time since I've had a man in my kitchen, you know. Your grandpa was an excellent cook. Nothing fancy, mind you, but I left it all up to him. He took care of me.'

I nod, watching Ed rummage in the bread bin. 'Yeah, it's nice to be taken care of. I think sometimes I forget to return the favour.'

Gubba and Grandpa Tom got married in the early sixties. She was twenty, he was thirty-five and apparently my great-grandmother didn't approve of the age difference. Gubba always said that he treated her like a queen, right up until his heart attack in 1989.

Gubba reaches over and places her hand on mine. 'It's hard getting old you know,' she says, 'because inside, in your heart, you don't age. You still feel and laugh and love exactly the way you always have. It's just the outside that reminds you that all this won't last forever. I'll never quite get used to seeing an old lady looking back at me in the mirror.'

I take her hand in mine and give it a little squeeze. Even though her skin might be thinner than it was, holding her hand still feels exactly as it did when I was a child.

'It's normal to want more, love,' she tells me. 'And it's normal to want time to yourself, to be by yourself. But all that time you wish you could have to yourself, Kate – one day you'll have it. One day there will be no work to do and no place to be and all you'll have is whatever time you have left. It's a much nicer place to be when you have someone to share it with.'

'Here we go!' Ed announces, placing more toast on Gubba's table. I'm not sure how much he has heard but the look on my face and my reluctance to let go of Gubba's hand make him do a one-eighty back into the kitchen.

'I love you, Gubba,' I tell her. 'And I'm sorry that Grandpa isn't here. I know you miss him.'

She nods. 'Sometimes I do. It'll be thirty-two years this year. It does get lonely, but Anthony in number twelve has been keeping me company.'

'Sorry, who?'

'Anthony. He's quite the charmer. He's seventy-six, from Trinidad. His legs are bad but the rest of him works—'

'Gubba!' I exclaim. I can't believe my ears.

'What?' she asks, munching her toast. 'I'm eighty-one Kate, I'm not dead. Life goes on, petal.'

'Ed!' I yell. 'Gubba's got a boyfriend. And he's younger!'

'What?' he asks, coming back through. 'Gubba? Is this true? Does Paula know about this?'

'Does she, heck,' Gubba replies. 'She'll scare the man off. One glare from her and he'll be wheeling himself out of here sharpish.'

Ed laughs the loudest because he knows better than anyone. When we first started hanging around together, Mum did everything but sit on the porch with a shotgun to ensure he behaved himself. I suppose part of that was due to her getting pregnant at sixteen. The rest was just her being a bossy cow, as usual.

'Well, my lips are sealed,' he says, sitting down beside me. 'But I think it's great. Good for you.'

She nods in agreement and goes back to her toast.

Mum and Gary show up just before one, bringing with them the shopping that I'd already agreed to pick up.

'It's fine,' Mum insists. 'Most of this will freeze. Damn, I've left Mum's meds in the car.'

'I'll get them,' Gary replies. 'No problem.'

'Oh, brilliant,' Paula responds. 'What would I do without you?'

'We really should get going,' I tell Gubba reluctantly. 'Are you sure there's nothing else we can do before we go?'

'I don't think so,' she replies. 'You get on your way.'

'Well OK, if you're sure. Take care and I'll call you soon,' I tell Gubba as we hug. 'And anything you need . . .'

'I know,' she says. 'It's been so lovely seeing the pair of you. Look after each other.'

'Bye, Gubba.'

We've already said our goodbyes to Mum and Gary, but I hug them again, anyway. I need it today.

I feel almost overwhelmed as we head back to the car. Until this visit, I'd never thought of Gubba as fragile, but now I realise just how short and fucking special our time together is – and not just with Gubba. My time with everyone. My time with Ed.

Ed

'You all right?' I ask Kate as we get in the car. She looks a million miles away.

'I think so,' she replies. 'It's just been a lot, you know.'

I nod and start the car, beginning our long drive home to London. To say our time here has been intense would be an understatement. Kate's handled everything brilliantly, though I had no doubt she would. She's the strongest woman I've ever known.

For the first part of the journey, all I can think about is what Gubba said to Kate and I'm fairly certain that she said it loudly enough so I could hear: *one day there will be no work to do and no place to be and all you'll have is whatever time you have left.*

I don't want to be alone when that happens, but I cannot envisage spending that time with anyone other than Kate – and that scares me.

We pull into motorway services to grab some lunch and fill up the car. I open my door to get out, but Kate stops me.

'It's nice, isn't it?' she remarks. 'What Mum said to Gary.'

'What? That she forgot Gubba's meds?'

She smiles. 'No . . .'

'Oh, that she doesn't know what she'd do without him?' I reply. 'Yeah, that was nice.'

She takes off her seatbelt and turns around to face me.

'It's that grateful feeling you get when you know there's someone there for you, no matter what. Someone who always has your back.'

'Yeah,' I agree. 'They're lucky to have each other. Shall we go and get—'

Kate places her hand on mine. 'That's the way I feel about you, Ed. Grateful. I'm so bloody thankful for you – you have no idea. I mean, why would you? I've made such a piss-poor show of it recently—'

'Kate, it's all right. You don't—'

'I do,' she says, softly. 'Please, just let me finish. I know I've screwed things up, but I can't lose you . . . and not because I don't want to be alone or because I get stupidly insecure. It's because you're my best friend.'

'You're not entirely to blame for all of this, Kate,' I admit. 'And these past few weeks have been horrendous, but at the end of the day, we still want different things.'

She turns her body towards me and sighs. 'Do you remember the day we came here to visit Tom for the first time?'

'Yeah,' I reply. 'We brought that stupid, creepy balloon with us. Didn't it end up floating through to your mum's room in the middle of the night?'

She laughs. 'Yes! She went at it with a pair of scissors. But there's something I never told you about that weekend, and I think it's only fair that I do.'

'OK . . .'

'Well, that weekend, I thought I was pregnant.'

'Are you serious?' I reply, closing the car door with a bang. 'Pregnant?'

'Yeah . . . I wasn't, obviously. My period was just late. But it scared the shit out of me. What it would mean for my career, for my future . . . for us.'

I sink back into my seat. I can't believe what I'm hearing. 'Jesus, Kate. That was years ago. Why didn't you tell me?'

'Because I knew how much you wanted kids!' she exclaims. 'God knows you made that abundantly clear so many times, and when I saw how great you were with Tom . . . I just knew if I told you, you'd want to keep it and I wasn't ready to have that discussion because I wasn't sure I wanted the same.'

The guilt begins to creep over me. She chose to deal with that alone, rather than talk to me about it. And I understand why. I'd begun planning our family long before I ever opened it up for discussion.

'I'm so sorry, Kate,' I say, staring at the floor. 'I should have been there for you.'

'Ed, it was eight years ago. So much has changed since then,' she says. 'Fuck, so much has changed since last month! When Gubba was ill and I saw the effect it had on my little brother . . . it was the first time I've ever felt properly protective. Maternal, almost. Does that make sense?'

I nod. 'It does.'

'All I wanted to do was make sure he was all right and shield him from the bad stuff as much as I possibly could. Same with my mum. I knew I had to put my own shit aside and step up. Fuck, what am I trying to say here?'

She pauses and takes a breath. 'Ed, I'm not sure I'll ever want to get married but having kids . . . with you? That's something I'm far less uncertain about.'

I feel a surge of excitement rise in my chest. 'You'll consider it?'

She nods. 'In a few years, you know – after I've retrained in human-rights law.'

'Really?'

'Really,' she replies. 'Oh god, don't cry – you'll set me off!'

I pull her to me and kiss her like it's the first time. Because bizarrely, that's exactly what it feels like.

'I've missed you so much,' I tell her. 'Come home, Kate. Please, just come home.'

EPILOGUE: DECEMBER 23RD

Kate

'Right, you go first. What did you get?'

'Are you ready for this?' I ask, slowly opening my bag to reveal a coronation chicken sandwich, so yellow, it's almost glowing. 'Ta-da! Beat that!'

Ed screws up his face. 'Jesus, did the person who made this also design your terrible trainers?'

'Very funny,' I reply. 'And no, I'm still not throwing them away.' Spending that entire day in my neon runners was the best thing that ever happened to my feet. I've never known such comfort. When I die, I intend to have them buried with me.

'Wait, what are those black things?' he asks, peering through the cellophane. He prods one with his finger.

'Sultanas, maybe?' I reply. 'Legless spider corpses? It's all part of the great mystery. Now, go on, show me yours.'

Ed shudders before revealing his choice of sandwich for the trip home. 'Triple cheese!' he proclaims. 'Here we have three different kinds of cheese on three kinds of equally dry bread. Guaranteed there's some onion involved some-where, just festering between two slices of stale brown.'

'Classy,' I respond, laughing. 'There's nothing like the stench of onion and cheese to make a packed train full of commuters warm to you with festive cheer.'

Just because Ed and I have decided to take the train home for Christmas this year, it doesn't mean we have to abandon our traditions completely. While we won't be stopping at any motorway service stations, we have preserved our sacred road-trip sandwich ritual. Well, apart from throwing the losing butty out the window.

The journey to Castleton this year will take us approxi-mately three hours, two train changes and a car ride, which, given last year's absolute shitshow, is totally worth it. Quite frankly, I'd rather walk barefoot over broken glass than go through that again. I'm sure we'll eventually get back to longer car journeys, but for now we're playing it safe.

Things are going well between Ed and me. Actually 'going well' doesn't quite cover it. A more accurate description would be more like 'fucking amazing' or 'astonishingly filthy'. It's not just the physical side that's back on track, however; emotionally, we're in a brilliant place. We've reconnected in a way that almost feels like it did when we were teenagers – the way we used to completely get each other but we weren't lazy or complacent about it. Back then it excited us. We revelled in it because it was ours and ours alone. Over the past year we've worked through our problems, some more successfully than others, but now, it feels like we're finally back at that place. That place where he can soothe me with music or where even the slightest touch can set off something explosive. It's a delightful place to be.

This Christmas we've decided it's time to throw out a few family traditions. No more separation. This year I want both families together for Christmas Day. I want us all to eat, open presents, sing carols and fall asleep in front of the television together. I want Tom to get to know Ed's family because they're my family, too. Yvonne and Chris have kindly opened their home to everyone and I feel like it's going to be the best Christmas ever. Ed and I also decided that Christmas this year just wouldn't be the same without the two people who helped ensure we stayed sane enough to see another one.

> Having to stop to charge the car for half an hour but should be in Castleton around six. Graham says he wants to go hiking so I'm dumping him as soon as we arrive L xx

I take out my laptop and try to log on to the free Wi-Fi, tutting every time it kicks me out, which is roughly every thirty seconds.

'Christ, it'd be quicker sending a carrier pigeon,' I mumble, typing in my email address for the umpteenth time.

'Aw, Kate . . . you promised,' Ed whinges. 'No work over Christmas, remember?'

'Ah, but it's not work,' I assure him. 'It's a good deed for a fellow classmate. I'm like the Christmas Fairy.'

'Hmm, that's not even a thing,' Ed replies.

'Yeah, and next you'll be telling me that Santa doesn't exist. I'm sending over some study notes to James; he missed the lecture on Tuesday and will surely fail his entire degree without them. See, I'm helping out my fellow man. This change of direction is paying off already.'

Leaving Parish Scott Taylor was easy – mainly because I was fired for walking out when Gubba got sick, but also because, deep down, I knew I was done. It just took me far too long to admit it. Surprisingly, Tara Mitchell-Brown also left Parish Scott Taylor when she found out why I was sacked. I was rather touched.

'That's bullshit. You did the right thing, I get it. My Nana Jean is a queen, babe. If she got sick, there's nothing that could keep me from her.'

Six months later, Tara was officially divorced, walking away with almost £2m, the house in Jesmond, a Range Rover HSE and even a brand-new foot spa, and I was enrolling at the London School of Economics to retrain in Human Rights Law. We still keep in touch, and she still throws one hell of a party.

Ed unwraps his sandwich and sniffs, his eyes darting

back to my phone as I type. 'James, huh? Who's James? Don't think you've mentioned him.'

I smirk. 'Haven't I? He's on my course. Bit older – maybe mid-thirties. He's super smart, really nice guy and . . . homely looking . . .'

Ed manages to laugh and blush at the same time. Although I'm now completely at peace with the whole Carly business, it doesn't hurt to wind him up every now and again.

Finally, I connect and email James my notes, wishing him and his husband a merry Christmas.

By the time we reach Leicester, Ed has officially won the sandwich battle, given that my neon atrocity is rather delicious, spider corpses and all. For his prize, I buy him an overpriced chickpea wrap, politely asking the onboard shop staff to burn and bury his three-cheese abomination.

'Heard anything from your dad?' Ed asks, taking his wrap.

I shake my head. 'Not a peep. He's officially disappeared again. I'm sure he'll resurface at some point.'

'Probably,' he replies. 'But I think it's more likely that Gubba killed him.'

I snort with laughter.

'Now, hear me out,' he continues. 'I've been thinking about this. She has that look about her, you know, like the matriarch in a crime movie. No one would suspect her. It's perfect.'

'Perfect, except for the fact that Gubba couldn't batter a fish,' I reply. 'Never mind kill someone. And we're hardly the Sopranos.'

'Look, if we get to Castleton and she's vanished with her passport, we'll know.'

I sit back and sigh. I haven't heard from my dad in nine weeks, which I should be used to by now, but I really thought he was making progress.

'Maybe I should just check the hospitals. I mean maybe he just went out for milk and—'

'Took the telly with him? Kate, you saw his flat. He cleared out the good stuff you bought him and left the rest for the council to deal with. I'm sure he'll turn up eventually but please don't let this ruin your Christmas.'

I nod and kiss Ed on his chickpea mouth. 'I won't. Promise.'

An hour later, we change trains at Sheffield, pleased that we'll be in Hope in around thirty minutes. Ed gives me the aisle seat, knowing the two coffees I've had will come back to haunt me soon. As we wait for the train to depart, Ed becomes fidgety.

'Music?' I suggest, offering Ed one of my earbuds. 'Might relax you.'

'Definitely,' he responds. 'Think I'm just a little nervous at everyone being together this year. What are we listening to?'

'Oh, just a little Christmas playlist I put together. No

biggie,' I reply. His face lights up. 'I knew there was a reason I loved you.'

I press shuffle, resting my head on Ed's shoulder as the opening bars from 'Merry Xmas Everybody' begin to play. The original version – I still hate the other one.

I'm half asleep when Ed gives me a nudge. 'Kate, we're here and it's snowing.'

I sit up and see a thick layer of snow on the platform. 'How pretty,' I remark, watching the snowflakes flurry past the window. 'It's been ages since we've had a white Christmas.'

'Think Gubba will be pleased?' Ed asks, laughing.

I start to laugh, too. Gubba loves the snow, almost as much as Tom does, and Tom would happily live in an igloo if we let him.

Grabbing our bags from the overhead storage area, Ed and I head outside to wait for his parents to pick us up, scrambling to put on our warm coats and gloves. We nip into the bus shelter, along with a large group of passengers, all of whom look as cold as I'm starting to feel.

'Any word from Graham and Lauren?' Ed asks, checking his phone. 'They should be checking into their hotel by now.'

'Nope,' I reply. 'I hope they're not stuck on the back roads. I'll text Lauren and let her know we're at the station.'

Ed puts his arms around me while I fire off a quick text to the missing duo. 'I like it like this,' he tells me. 'When it's all white and quiet. Kind of romantic, don't you think?'

'Hmm . . . maybe you can write about it for one of your open-mic nights?' I tease. 'Maybe play it on the clarinet?'

'I have feelings, you know,' he says, feigning upset.

'You know I'm only joking,' I reply. 'Your open-mic nights are the highlight of my week. I feel like a groupie. Why are you looking at me like that? Is my hair weird?'

He takes a deep breath. Shit, did I actually offend him?

'Kate . . . God, I was going to wait to do this but, fuck it.'

He goes down on one knee.

'Ed, what the hell—'

'Kate Ward . . . will you *not* marry me?'

I pause. 'Sorry, what?'

'Will you not marry me?' he repeats, almost sounding unsure of his own words.

I'm so confused. 'Ed, I'm already not married to you,' I say through gritted teeth. 'Can you please get up? Everyone's staring . . .'

'I know,' he replies, his knee still firmly planted in the snow. 'But if we can't do the whole ceremony, the vows and the official-piece-of-paper rigmarole, that's fine – I can live with that. But what I can't live with is not proving to you just how committed I am to you. To us. I need that.'

He reaches into his backpack and pulls out a small red box. Before I have a chance to gasp, the woman to my right does it for me.

'So forget about the marriage, but let me do the ring,'

he says. 'Let me do the honeymoon. Let's get a mortgage and send tacky joint Christmas cards and buy a family SUV with plenty of space for the dog we'll adopt. If you'll agree not to marry me, I promise I'll spend the rest of my life being the best damn non-husband you've ever seen.'

I can't stop grinning. This is the best non-proposal I've ever heard. It's the only non-proposal I've ever heard.

'Yes,' I reply, almost as surprised at my response as Ed is.

'Yes?' he questions, his eyebrows shooting upwards. 'You're saying yes?'

'Yes, I will not marry you!' I yell, much to the amusement and confusion of everyone around us.

He places the ring on my finger, and I squeal. It's green onyx, just like the earrings I wanted last Christmas. He remembered. I don't know whether to laugh or cry, so instead I throw my arms around him and do both.

'I love you so much,' I tell him. 'I'm going to be the best non-wife ever!'

'I love you, too,' he says, placing his hands on my face, then kissing me, so softly, I fear I might melt.

'Eww, they're kissing!'

I pull my face away from Ed to see Tom, in bright green wellies, making a beeline for us, just as his snowball hits my leg.

'What the . . .' Everyone is here, not just Ed's parents: Mum, Gary, even Gubba. I wave my newly not-engaged hand towards everyone like the Queen.

'Well, you did say you wanted a joint Christmas this year,' Ed remarks. 'Everyone together in one place.'

'Yeah, I didn't mean the station car park, Ed.'

'Think they saw all that?' he asks.

'Yep,' I reply. 'One hundred per cent. Look at your mum's face – she's about to implode.'

He smiles and takes a deep breath. 'OK. Ready to go and confuse the shit out of everyone?'

'Definitely,' I reply. 'We can . . .' My words are muffled by a second snowball which lands squarely on the side of my face.

Tom laughs loudly. 'Yeah! You got her, Gubba!'

Gubba? I wipe my face to see Gubba laughing hysterically.

Ed and I take cover behind the bus which pulls up to collect the rest of the passengers and begin scooping up snow, ready to pelt the living daylights out of an elderly woman and a young boy. However, Ed's dad lands one on Gary and knocks his hat off which makes me roar with laughter.

As I watch our families begin their first proper Christmas together with a snowball fight, I can't help but smile. Of all the fights I've had at Christmas, this is by far my favourite.

ACKNOWLEDGEMENTS

Firstly, a huge thank you to my editor Florence Hare for being so patient and supportive, along with all the staff from Quercus who worked on the book with me. Also to my agent Kerry Glencorse and everyone at Susanna Lea Associates. I'm grateful to you all.

A huge thank you to Mum, Dad, Claudia, Matias and baby Valentina for being so bloody wonderful and of course, my daughter Olivia who never complains when I sing in the car.

Special thanks to Debbie Connor for your musical knowledge and to Nicola for reminding me that fun still exists, even with a walking stick.